The Keeper and the Alabaster Chalice

The Keeper and the Alabaster Chalice © 2013 by Paige W. Pendleton

The Keeper

and the
Alabaster
Chalice

BOOK II OF THE BLACK LEDGE SERIES

Paige W. Pendleton

Illustrations by Thomas Block

PIG WING PRESS

Dedication

For My Parents David and Kathleen Waterman
Thank you for believing in magic, and me.

Acknowledgements

THOMAS BLOCK, MAGICAL CREATIONS ASIDE, MY APPRECIA-
tion for your enthusiasm, support, many kindnesses comes from
the bottom of my heart. Thank you.

Disclaimer: Anything wrong with this book is not Robb
Grindstaff's fault.

I'm kidding, but my gratitude for all Robb does (and teaches
me) is sincere. Thank you.

To Judy Beatty, who guides and shapes so gently, and so darn
fast, thank you.

To Brion Sausser at Book Creatives. You rock. Start to finish.
Thank you so much.

To the members of the IC: Every day is nicer because of you.
Especially Wednesdays.

To Audrey Lane, my target audience Beta Reader and a
crackerjack critquer.

I have the best promo team, and friends: Apryl Grindle,
Shirley Remson, Tina Pendleton, Shelly Wilbur, Heidi Baker,
Martha Flint, Jen Blood, Ally Jordan, Bonnie Brooks, Cheryl
Fallon, and Amanda Phillips. For your unflagging support and
shameless plugs, I thank you.

For Chris Morley, who brightens each day, transatlantically.

Floyd won't let me forget to thank Ron Dyer for always
knowing what "day" it is.

For the laughter: Pele. Jonathan. Look. You're forever

immortalized.

Richard Gray, because he'll harass me if I don't.

Vern. Mine, not Vernon Baker's. Tap, tap, tap, man. xox

My sister, Hillary, who is wonderful. I love you. Toad Thief.

I thank, deeply and with love, my husband Richard and my wonderful daughters, Ellie and Frances. It bears repeating, and often.

Prologue

RESTLESS, MOTTE SHIFTED FROM ONE LEG TO THE OTHER, HER talons gouging the granite as she settled on the pediment.

The Ley Lines sang to her. They sang of what had been, what was, and what was yet to be. Songs, older than time, of love, joy, and loss, dwelled in Motte's heart, and she recognized what had been prophesied had come to pass.

He'd bonded with the child. It was foretold, and so it would be.

Chapter One

THE MOORED BOATS POINTED TOWARD THE MOUTH OF THE harbor as if nosing a southeasterly wind, but that was only an illusion. All was still and silent in the morning sunshine. Not a breath of air stirred.

The boat drifted, and Jack let out an aggravated sigh. Sails hung limp and motionless, ignoring his every effort to fill them. "We could swim faster than this."

Sounded like a good idea to Eleanor. The cockpit felt like a frying pan, but she kept that observation to herself. She leaned back, dangled her arm over the side, and trailed her fingers through the cold water.

An eider popped up beside the hull, startling a laugh from Eleanor. That, in turn, startled the eider, and it dove back under the water.

"Stupid bird," Jack muttered.

A crow landed on the boat's rail. "Watch yourself, young man."

"Good morning, Agnes," Eleanor greeted the sleek, black bird in a singsong voice, amused the crow had overheard Jack's comment and he faced her displeasure. "Don't mind Jack. He's just frustrated. The high seas beckon and he can't even make it out of the harbor."

"Quiet, Swabbie." Jack smiled sheepishly at the crow. "Sorry, Agnes."

The crow's eyes narrowed for a split second, then she ruffled her feathers and said, "Camedon wants to see you when you come in." Her short tone revealed her annoyance, but Eleanor suspected it was her discomfort with being on a boat, more than what Jack said.

"Why didn't he just come find us?" asked Jack.

Agnes stared at Jack for several moments, considering her answer. Finally she said, "He's not able to come to you himself."

Dread crept into Eleanor's stomach. Had something happened?

Agnes cleared her throat, looked around, and said in a low voice, "He gets seasick."

Jack cracked up. "You're kidding!"

"Shhh!" The crow hissed, but Jack ignored her disapproval, tickled with that knowledge.

His laughter was contagious and Eleanor had a difficult time keeping a straight face under Agnes's scrutiny. But it was funny, and Eleanor suspected even Camedon would think so. A green Keeper—the ridiculous image clashed with the Keeper's dignified position.

They'd met Camedon in a cave on the beach. He was magical, and revealed an entire Realm of the world—one with Elves, Dwarves, Fairies, Sprites, and other fantastical beings and creatures. The things of fairy tales and legends, except Eleanor knew now that they weren't just fairy tales and legends.

Jack continued to chortle, and asked Agnes, "Have you told Rob?"

"I stopped at Black Ledge and told your brother first." The crow twitched her head toward shore.

Eleanor's gaze moved to their home overlooking the harbor. Every kid in Camden was familiar with the old place. Abandoned for decades, it was the favorite setting for ghost stories and dares on Halloween night. While it no longer looked haunted and creepy, it was still hard to believe it was now their home.

"What's up?" asked Jack.

"I think he just wanted to visit." The crow looked past Eleanor to the water. "Oh. Hello, Seaton."

A head broke the surface and large brown eyes studied them. The seal waggled his whiskers at Agnes.

"Hullo, luv," the seal said in a rough, gravelly voice. "How are you this fine morning? Who're your friends?"

"Jack and Eleanor Driscoll," Agnes said. "They moved into Black Ledge a few weeks ago. They are *aware.*"

"Gathered that. Not very often I see you sailing." He splashed water with his snout toward Agnes. She stepped back to avoid getting wet, and proved his point. He greeted Jack and Eleanor, "Hullo. Pleased to meet ya."

"Hi," Eleanor and Jack said at the same time.

"Hold that thought." The seal disappeared with a splash.

Jack and Eleanor looked at Agnes, questioning, but before she could answer, Seaton's head popped back up. He gulped, smacking his lips around a mackerel tail.

"Mackerel're in," he told them.

"Yeah, I saw fireflies last night," Jack agreed.

"There ya go. When you see fireflies, you know the mackerel're in." Seaton nodded with approval. Jack had just passed some sort of test.

"What are you doing this morning, Seaton?" Agnes asked.

"Well, seeing you this morning is what you might call a fort-tu-it-tuss circumstance. I need to speak with Camedon."

"I'm not his messenger," Agnes said.

"Aw, come on, Aggie. You know I can't very well go find

him." He waggled his whiskers at her again, trying to gain her good favor.

"If I see him, I'll let him know," the crow informed him, promising nothing. "And don't call me Aggie."

"Righto, doll. Well, best be off. Haven't had second breakfast yet. Nice to meet ya." He bobbed his head at the kids, and submerged.

"*Doll* doesn't really work for me, either," Agnes muttered.

"This is a drag, Jack. Why don't we bag it until there's some wind? At this rate we'll be lucky to clear The Graves by noon," Eleanor said, indicating the deadly ledges beyond the harbor with a jerk of her head.

Jack sighed, disappointed. "I s'pose. It'll take us an hour to even get back to the mooring." Then he brightened. "But you know, that seal may be onto something with this second breakfast stuff."

"Cutting back to two breakfasts a day?"

"Quiet, Swabbie," he growled in his most ferocious pirate voice. "Is there an oar below?" He indicated the space beneath the boat's deck.

Eleanor pulled out an oar and handed it to him.

"It might work better if you stood on the bow," he said.

"Me?"

"My boat. You crew."

"No. This boat belongs to all of us."

"Well, I'm captain today. Come on, Eller. You're closer."

Eleanor gave him an annoyed look, but she climbed onto the bow, stepping over the slack jib lines and pushing the sail out of her way in an exaggerated fashion. "Take it down, at least, would you?"

"Sure." He reached forward, uncleated the jib halyard, and

let it go. The sail collapsed on top of her.

"Jack!" Eleanor struggled under the sail. "Knock it off or I'll swim in and leave you here."

"Keep it up, young man, and you're apt to have a mutiny on your hands," Agnes said.

The low thrum of a motor grew louder. As it grew closer, Jack and Eleanor recognized their older brother Rob and little sister Flora in the family's whaler.

"Hey!" Eleanor waved them in.

Rob did a wide arc and pulled alongside the sailboat, slowing the whaler at just the right second. "You guys want a tow? Hey, Agnes."

"No," Eleanor said, still trying to furl the sail and get it out of her way. "I want you to take me in and we'll leave Jack here."

"Is this what they call *pleasure boating*?" Rob asked. "Better toss a line, Flora."

Flora did, and Eleanor caught it and fed it through the chock, but didn't cleat it.

"You guys want to go to the mooring or do you want to leave the boat on the dock?" Rob asked.

"Mooring." Eleanor was done sailing for the day.

"Dock." Jack wasn't.

Rob waited for them to decide.

"Fine. The dock," Eleanor said. "Maybe you can shanghai Flora into servitude. I'm going riding."

"I'll go sailing later, Jackie," Flora piped up, and Jack shot a triumphant smile at Eleanor.

"Agnes told you we have to see Camedon?" Rob said.

Jack grinned. "Old Captain Cam? Yup."

Agnes looked mortified. "Don't you say anything, Jack Driscoll."

"Not me, Agnes." Jack pretended to lock his lips and throw the key over his shoulder.

Seaton's head popped up. "Oops, almost forgot."

He had something in his mouth, and he tossed it onto the boat's deck. Eleanor picked it up. It had slime on it. She handed it to Jack. He didn't mind slime.

Jack twisted it every which way, but it was so covered in barnacles it was impossible to identify. "What's this?"

"Give it to Camedon, would you? Tell him it's from Doris." The seal disappeared. Quickly.

Chapter Two

CAMEDON CAST AN ADMIRING GLANCE AROUND THE LIBRARY. "Your mother has outdone herself. No one would believe this was the same house."

"Where do *you* live?" asked Jack. He sat sideways in a chair beside the fireplace, legs over one arm.

Eleanor hoped her mother would walk in.

Camedon simply smiled. "It's a secret."

Before Jack could push, Rob interrupted. "Agnes said you wanted to see us."

"I'd like to borrow the pendants Gunnr made." Camedon walked to one of the sofas. He adjusted the elegant cloak that identified him as a Keeper of the Realm, and sat. "The two you found? Queen Solvanha and King Vitr would like to examine them. Gunnr was fine with it. Interesting magic—a combination of both the Dwarves' and Elven magics."

"Oh! We met a seal named Seaton this morning," Eleanor told him, and Camedon's face broke into a grin.

"How is old Seaton?" Camedon asked. "Mackerel in yet? I saw fireflies last night."

"They are! He ate one while he was talking to us," Jack said. At Rob's confused look Jack explained, "We discussed firefly-mackerel relativity."

"Hard to talk to Seaton when the mackerel are running," Camedon said. "Hard to talk to him anyway—he gets distracted—but it's especially hard to talk to him when the mackerel are running. They're his favorites, all greasy and extra fishy."

"He asked Agnes to tell you he'd like a word," Jack said. "You know," he added, pretending to have an idea, "I'd be happy to take you sailing this afternoon if we get some wind, and we could find him. He gave us something, too. Said to tell you it was from Doris. Hang on, I left it in the foyer."

Jack ran out of the room and came back holding the crusty lump. He handed it to the Keeper.

"Doris? Are you *sure* he said Doris?"

"I think so. It was Doris, wasn't it, El?"

"Yeah," Eleanor agreed.

Camedon frowned. "I'll just pop over to his rock. I can't sail this afternoon, Jack. Another time, perhaps."

The decline was artful, but a decline it was. Eleanor and Jack shared a grin.

Rob eyed Jack, suspicious of Jack's helpfulness, but changed the subject. "Before you go, we have to talk about the Elven *Guards.*" Rob made quote signs with his fingers as he said 'guards.'

Camedon raised his hands in protest. "Not my department. You have to speak with Queen Solvanha."

Though Black Point, the peninsula on which the Driscoll's house sat, was protected, the Elven Queen decided the kids needed guards after Eleanor had been abducted by a Noctivagus. The queen had assigned members of the Elven Guard to accompany the kids if they left Black Point.

"You can speak with her, can't you?" Rob said.

"I could, but I'm not going to. Even if I did, it wouldn't do any good. She won't be swayed. Not after what happened to Eleanor. Give it a few weeks, at least until we know things have settled down a bit. Curiosity about you is high right now. Let the

Realm become accustomed to your presence, and you to it, and then we'll see. It makes your parents feel better. Look, I know you feel as if you have a babysitter, and that chafes at your age, but Flora's only eight."

"But we have the pendants Gunnr gave us," Jack reminded him, taking a small, felt bag from his pocket. He opened the drawstring and dumped a small star on a chain into his hand. Perfect replicas of the Älvkors and Rune Stone, the pendants were embued with magic that enabled the kids to speak with the Night Elf mentally, in the Elven way.

"That's a reasonable point, Jack. I'll remind her of it when we address this again." Placating tone aside, it was obvious the Keeper wasn't going to change his mind.

Neither Rob nor Jack appeared thrilled.

"They never say anything," Jack grumbled. "Just follow us. Watching."

"Who? The Elven Guards?"

"Yeah. They just hang around looking like someone died."

"They're guards, Jack." Camedon smiled. "They're not here for a play date."

"I'll get the pendants," Rob said, and left.

Jack had another question. "Camedon?"

"Yes?"

"So we met Seaton—never really thought about sea creatures. Can we understand fish, too?"

"Only if you put your head under the water."

Jack rolled his eyes. "I'm serious."

"So was I."

"I want to see Seaton again," Flora said.

"I'm sure you will," Camedon said. "Seaton is usually hanging around the harbor. Keeps an eye on the comings and goings from his rock by the lighthouse. Not much happens in the harbor that Seaton isn't aware of."

Rob came back into the library, the pendants hanging from his left hand. "Got 'em."

The Keeper took them and put them in his vest pocket. "I'll get these back to you when Queen Solvanha and King Vitr are through examining them. I think your parents should wear them."

Jack grinned. "You can tell them that. Here you go. Talk to a vampire anytime you want."

"Shut up, Jack," Eleanor said.

"Just kidding."

"Gunnr's not a vampire. He's a Night Elf."

"Simmer down. I was just joshing."

Eleanor's eyes narrowed, and Rob interrupted. "Enough, you guys. Flora, you and I should go sailing and leave these two here."

"My boat," Jack said.

"It isn't your boat, Jackie," Flora corrected him.

"It is today. I've laid claim. Just waiting for fair winds to fill me sails."

Camedon stood. "Well, thanks for these. Best find Seaton before he forgets what he wanted."

He vanished with the loud *POP* that accompanied his magical entrances and exits.

Chapter Three

JACK SULKED IN THE BOW OF THE WHALER. "STILL NO WIND."

"Give it a rest, would you?" Even Rob was sick of Jack's whining. "This is faster anyway. Let's see if we can find Seaton's rock. I think it's beside Curtis Island."

"The Light House?"

"Yeah, Camedon said he likes keeping an eye on the comings and goings—even when he's snoozing."

The lighthouse sat on a small island, surrounded by rocks and ledges, at the mouth of the harbor. Boats passed the light as they entered and exited the harbor in the carefully marked channel. The whaler, though, didn't draw much water, and Rob was able to cut straight across to the island. Rob slowed as he approached the island and the kids looked for the seal.

Flora pointed at a large gray mass on the ledges. "Is that him?"

Rob picked his way through the rocks close to the shore. The seaweed in the shallows dragged along the bottom of the boat. As they neared, they could make out a figure sitting in a hollow below the seal.

"Camedon's with him," Eleanor said.

"Huh." Rob nosed the boat to the ledge.

Jack waved. "Hey."

Camedon beckoned them closer. "I suspected you'd be along. Seaton, you've met Jack and Eleanor, and these are the other two Driscolls, Rob and Flora."

"Pleased to make yer 'quaintance." The seal waggled his whiskers.

"Hi! Hi!" Flora said, simply beside herself. She scrambled to the side of the whaler to get closer, and the boat tipped. Eleanor moved quickly to the other side to compensate.

The seal let out a yawn. "Camedon caught me here just afore me morning nap. Always have one after second breakfast, see? When the sun gets high."

Something rose from the water and pulled itself onto the rock next to Seaton and Camedon.

"Useless layabout," it croaked.

Flora shrank back into the boat, recoiling from the creature.

The creature had gray hair snarled with clumps of seaweed and pale green skin. Its bulging eyes were too large for its wrinkled face, and the irises were opalescent in color. As the rest of it emerged from the water, its large fish-like tail became visible.

"And you're just a mean old woman, Doris. Why are you here? I got your message to Camedon, and gave him the—"

"Shut up, you idiot," she hissed.

"Told you," Seaton said to Camedon.

Camedon's smile broadened. "Doris! So good to see you. How long has it been?"

"Not long enough. I hate coming to the surface. Did you get it?"

"Yes, I did, but what is it?"

"I'd rather not say. It's your problem now. Keep it on land. It's too dangerous to leave in the sea. Give it to a museum, I don't care, but get rid of it," she told him, and made for the water.

"Wait—"

"No," she said. "It's cursed, and no good can come of it. Get it out of my waters."

"Told you," Seaton said to the Keeper.

"Doris. Surely you understand the predicament I'm in. I

need to know—"

"No, you don't. Throw it in a hole for all I care. Just get rid of it."

She slid into the water and disappeared.

"Told you," Seaton said again.

Camedon let out a sigh. "Get her back," he instructed the seal.

"What? We just got her to leave. Whatcha want her back fer?"

"I have to talk to her. Go get her."

The seal grumbled as he slid down the rocks.

Eleanor thought she heard the words 'mean old woman.'

"And ask nicely," the Keeper reminded the seal as he slid beneath the waves.

"Who was that?" Jack got the question out first.

"Doris. The Acadian Water Witch."

"Who's she?"

"You might call her a mermaid. She's lives out on Lime Island," Camedon said, pointing toward the bay.

"I thought mermaids were pretty," Jack said.

Eleanor kicked him.

"What? She's horrid."

"Doris … how should I put this? Doris likes her privacy," Camedon said. His diplomacy wasn't lost on the kids. She didn't like anyone.

The witch's head emerged. "What now?" Hanks of hair floated on the surface around her head. It was quite gruesome.

Camedon tried reason. "Doris, I don't even know what this thing is."

"You don't need to know what it is! Just dispose of it. That's it. Will you or won't you?" The witch leveled her creepy eyes at the Keeper.

"Where did it come from?" Camedon asked.

She studied him, a frown on her face. Finally she said, "The wreck of the Rachel Parker."

"The Rachel Parker? That went down centuries ago. What exactly is this thing, Doris?" Camedon frowned and Eleanor suspected he already knew he wasn't going to like the answer.

"I don't want to tell you," she said, her eyes averted.

Camedon didn't reply. Again, he waited.

"Fine. It's the Alabaster Chalice," she answered in a low voice.

Camedon's face froze.

Seaton let out a whistle.

Doris kept her eyes downcast.

The kids didn't know which one to look at.

Finally Camedon spoke. "You were going to have me *dispose* of the Alabaster Chalice? *Throw in a hole?* Doris. What were you thinking? How long have you had this?"

"Too long, and I'm done. I don't want it lying around my cave anymore. Someone told him and he's on his way here. You have to take it, Camedon."

"Doris. Good Heavens. You had to know he'd come someday, and he'd be furious."

"Well, he should have taken better care of it," the witch said.

Eleanor could have sworn she heard her say under her breath, "And me," as her head sunk below the surface again.

Camedon stared at the spot, flabbergasted.

"Told you." Seaton broke the silence.

Camedon ignored him. "Well. This is a fine kettle of fish."

Eleanor might have laughed at the pun if he hadn't looked so discouraged. He rubbed his face, and Eleanor could tell he was flummoxed.

"Mean old woman. She's just a mean old woman. Ugly, too," Seaton went on, oblivious to the deflated expression on the Keeper's face.

"What's the Alabaster Chalice?" Rob asked.

"A headache." The Keeper let out a long sigh, and turned to

THE KEEPER AND THE ALABASTER CHALICE

the kids. "The Alabaster Chalice is an artifact with a tangled history. A Dwarven artifact, capable of purifying one of the four elements. It's a vessel, carved from alabaster. Beautiful and ancient."

Rob asked, "Dwarves? Then why would she have it?"

"I know some of it, the rest I can guess. As you know, Dwarves have a magic with things, and iron, in particular, is precious to them. It has properties they value—one being protection. You've heard the folklore. Cemeteries are surrounded by an iron fence to contain the souls of the dead. An iron horse shoe nailed to a door wards off bad spirits. Burying an iron knife under the entrance to one's home keeps witches from entering—"

"I need a knife," Seaton grumbled, eyeing the spot where Doris had disappeared.

Camedon ignored him and went on. "The Dwarves carved the Chalice from a special piece of alabaster. A piece beautifully colored by iron deposits. Form follows function, and while it was beautiful the iron also served a purpose beyond decoration. The purpose of protection. Purification."

"What was it protecting?"

"Water."

Jack's frowned. "Water?"

The Keeper explained, "There are four elements of the Olde Magyk. Earth, Air, Fire, and Water. Each is represented by an artifact capable of purifying that substance to its elemental form—no other contaminants. Each purified element is also a restorative. Liquid in the Alabaster Chalice becomes the element water, and has strong restorative properties."

"You mean like an elixir?" Rob asked.

"Yes, just like an elixir. Each element has powerful properties, but when combined? One is capable of practicing the Olde Magyk. If one controlled all four, and knew how, one could even affect the fifth element, the most nebulous and fluid, Time."

"But you said once no one messes around with Time."

A strange look passed over Camedon's face. "It's terribly dangerous, and usually disastrous."

"Anything else you want to share with us?" asked Jack. "Armageddon? The apocalypse? A cataclysmic devastation of the world? Anything?"

"Knock it off, Jack," Eleanor said.

"After the ritual sacrifice, the artifacts of the Four Elements were separated and given to different beings to be safeguarded. The Undine, Beings of the Waters, were charged with the Alabaster Chalice. It's been passed through history from each reigning monarch to the next."

"So where does Doris fit into this?" Rob asked.

"Doris was once young, and like all young Beings tend to do, she fell in love."

"That's frightening," Jack said.

Camedon smiled. "The object of her affection was the Undine Prince, Newlin, and while he returned her affection, his family did not. They were unwilling to accept a Water Witch as a suitable match for the heir to the Undine throne. Unable to sway his family, Newlin eventually acquiesced to his family's wishes. Doris was terribly hurt, and then her hurt became bitterness. How the Alabaster Chalice came to be on the Rachel Parker I don't know, but being of such import to Newlin, heir to the Undine throne, Doris pirated it from the wreck and held on to it. Either to keep it safe or to get even. Or maybe both."

The creature had gray hair snarled with clumps of seaweed and pale green skin.

Chapter Four

PATTERS SAT ON THE PORCH STEPS, WAITING. SHE STOOD AS the kids approached.

"You need to come to the barn. I don't know where he came from, but he cannot stay." The cat was vexed.

"Who?" Rob asked.

"The Hob. We cannot have a Hob in the barn. It's my barn. He can't stay."

"Slow down. What's a Hob?" Eleanor asked the cat.

"A pest, that's what. He has to go. I will *not* share the barn with a Hob. It's too much to ask. He's torn the place apart. He's moving everything around. Cleaning—the dust is all stirred up. You can't even breathe in there! He's oiling the tack and it's strewn everywhere. He's restacking the hay—it's chaos. And Nickerson will be down soon!"

That got the kids attention. Nickerson, Sam Nickerson, their mother's childhood riding instructor, lived in the carriage house and took care of the barn and the horses. He was *unaware* of the Beings of the Realm.

They started for the barn.

"Wait. Does this Hob clean stalls?" asked Jack.

No one answered him. He sighed and followed.

The Hob was three and a half feet tall, sturdy, and suitably attired in a red plaid shirt and overalls. Sporting a straw hat and whistling, he stopped what he was doing when he saw the children approaching.

"Howdy! I fig-urred I'd start in the barn," he greeted them in an overly affected drawl.

"Hi. Who're you?" Eleanor asked.

"I'm Floyd," he announced. Proudly, as if she should have heard of him.

"And what brings you here?" Rob asked.

"Wa-l-l-l," Floyd began, "there's life here again. Y'all need a Hob to keep the place tiptop." He waggled his eyebrows, smiled a salesman's smile, and jerked his thumb at his own chest. "I'm your Hob. I'll have this place sparkling faster than you kin shake a stick. Then I'll hit the house. Hobs, see, are better 'n Goblins, Tomtes, or Brownies. Tomte's are prickly, peevish types. They're all hairy, too. And Brownies are housebound. I can work inside or out. House, barn, makes no nevermind to me."

"We have a Goblin," Patters informed him. "And Brownies."

"We do?" The kids all asked at the same time, surprised.

"Yes. In the house where they belong. This barn is already being looked after. By me. Your services are not needed," she dismissed the Hob.

"Now, now. Let's not be too hasty. I think you'll find my comp'ny to yer likin'," he said.

"And knock off that ridiculous accent," Patters snapped. "I know you speak properly. No, we're fine here. You may move along."

"Too late, honey. I did the ritual."

Patter's eyes narrowed and she hissed. "You stay out of my way. And be discreet—we have Humans who aren't *aware*," she said.

"Wait. What ritual?" Rob asked.

"The Hob ritual. When we take a new residence, we perform a ritual pledging our service and fealty. We choose a stone from the property and swear allegiance, and we must carry the stone at all times. I have mine here on my watch fob." He lifted a pocket watch from the front of his overalls and showed it to the kids. "It also renews our magic. A Hob with no home has faulty magic. But the rule is clear. One Hob family per residence. If a ritual has already been performed by a residing Hob, the squatter Hob gets their fingers singed when he or she tries to perform the ritual. Smarts, too," he added, rubbing his fingers with a frown. He gave Patters a triumphant look. "So it's a done deal. I'm here to stay."

Patters turned to the kids and said, "You'll regret this. You'll see. Before you know it, he'll be Lord of The Manor." She stomped off, tail stiff in the air.

"I'd give Patters space if I were you," Jack suggested, grinning. "You clean stalls, right?"

"I do everything. Even windows."

"Wood?" Rob asked.

"Stop, you guys," Eleanor interrupted. "Floyd, Patters is right. We have people around who aren't *aware.*"

"You won't even know I'm here. I'll have this barn put to rights in no time, and then I'll see to the house. After I get settled in, I'll go back to my regular schedule. I'm an early riser, and nap in the late morning."

"The carriage house …" Flora reminded them.

"Yeah, leave the carriage house be. Nickerson lives there," Rob said, still grinning.

"The horses?" Eleanor asked.

"Oh," the Hob waved his hand. "No worries there. We've already met. Off with you now. I've work to do. Idle hands are the devil's workshop."

Patters snorted from somewhere near the tack room.

"I'm going riding," Eleanor announced.

"Where you headed? " Rob asked.

"The lake. It's hot."

"Can I come?" Flora asked.

"You were going to come sailing," Jack reminded her.

"What's the matter, Captain Bligh?" Eleanor asked. "Losing

more crew? You guys work it out. I'm going swimming. I don't care who comes."

She went out to the pasture and climbed the fence. The horses were on the other side of the field, and they trotted over when they spied her. She jumped down and opened the gate for her palomino, Ginger.

"We're all going," Jack conceded from behind her.

"Yessuh! Let's go swimming." Ringo trotted to him.

Eleanor grinned. "You're getting your Maine accent down, Ringo."

Rob took Sargent, the large hunter, by the halter and led him through the gate. Flora took her pony, Willow.

Hala, the Arabian mare their mother rode, and Mack, the chestnut gelding, were left in the pasture.

"What will we be needing for tack this afternoon, young mistresses and masters?" Floyd asked from the doorway of the barn.

Jack smirked at Rob. "This is going to work out just fine."

Eleanor led Ginger into the barn. "Nothing, Floyd. We can get our own tack. *Can't we*, Jack?"

"Just bridles, El? If we're swimming?" Flora asked.

"Yeah, I'm going bareback."

The kids slipped bridles on each of their horses and took turns at the mounting block in front of the barn. They left the stable yard and started down the point road.

"Where were you thinking? I don't really want to go to Barrett's Cove," Rob said, referring to the public beach on the lake. "Too many people."

"The river?" Eleanor suggested. "Just this side of the East Dam? It's hard sand—good bottom, no muck, and there won't be many people, if any."

"I wish we were there already," Flora said.

"Too hot to hurry," Rob told her.

"You guys met Floyd?" Eleanor asked the horses.

"Odd little fellow. Hobs are, in general," Sargent said.

"Patters wasn't impressed," Eleanor said.

"Wahl, cats tend to be purdy possessive of their barns," Ringo said.

"Tough. He does chores," Jack said.

"You know Mum and Dad will zero that right out," Eleanor told him.

"When they find out," Jack said. "But did you catch what Patters said about the Brownies? I didn't know we had Brownies."

"You wouldn't," Sargent explained. "Brownies work at night, usually after everyone is asleep. They're busy. Not chatty. Keep to themselves. They're bound to the house they work in and you usually find them living in or close to the kitchens."

Rob yelled, "Look out!" He crouched low on Sargent's withers, avoiding a flock of swooping birds. They fluttered around their heads, wings humming.

A chorus of high-pitched voices filled the air. "Hello!"

Sargent groaned. "Oh no. Pyskes!"

Eleanor ducked. "Huh?" At least fifty hummingbird-sized things darted all around, buzzing and chattering. She resisted the urge to swat the little bodies away from her face.

"Pyskes. I thought you didn't have any here. I should have known it was too good to be true." Ringo's head dropped. He sounded as discouraged as Sargent.

Jack dodged one that zoomed past his head. "What are Pyskes?"

"A nuisance," Willow told them. "Pyske infestations plague stables. They love horses. Follow us everywhere. The children play in our manes, leaving terrible tangles. They nest in the hay. Sprinkle dust everywhere." Willow sneezed as a shower of dust sprinkled over her.

They fluttered around their heads, wings humming.

"You don't say," Rob said in a dry tone, gently pushing away a persistent one flapping by his face, fanning thick dust with his other hand.

A sharp whistle cut the air and the smaller Pyskes backed off a bit. Two larger ones flew down and hovered in front of Rob and Sargent.

"Hello, Noble Equines!" The larger of the two Pyskes greeted the horses exuberantly, and bowed to each, in turn. His wings hummed so fast they were barely visible. "My name is Felix. This is my wife, Trinket, and our children. So happy to hear the stable at Black Ledge is alive again! And here we are! Honored to be the first family to arrive and claim the stable. Be *the* First Family of the Stable."

"Did someone hang a vacancy sign at the end of the point road?" asked Jack, incredulous. "Hobs, Pyskes, Brownies, Witches ... what next?"

"Elves?" Baelhar, one of the Elven Guard, materialized on the road, smiling.

Jack sighed. "I knew it."

"'Fraid so, Jack. You're being invaded, my friend. Beings of the Realm are excited Black Ledge has Humans in residence again, and are curious. The queen foresaw this, so until she says we needn't, we're your shadows. Chin up. Things will simmer down." The Elf looked around, his smile growing. "Hello, Pyskes."

"Pyskes are good security," Willow said.

"Really?" Rob asked.

"Oh, yes. They patrol their property constantly. Pyskes are hyperactive, have high metabolisms, and need to keep busy. They're observant, too."

A calculating expression crossed Jack's face. "Good enough security to get rid of our guards?"

Baelhar shrugged. "Maybe. We'll see. Willow is right. With a flock of Pyskes, you probably don't need protection on the point. Excellent security." He smiled and added, "Then again, you might decide guards aren't so bad."

The Elf disappeared again, but the kids knew he and the rest of the guards were still present, and would stay with them.

Two of the Pyske children landed on Sargent's neck and lifted pieces of his mane. They darted to and fro, over and under, braiding. Sargent jerked his head up, rattling his curb chain. "Now see here. It isn't worth it. Pyskes are a dratted nuisance." The large hunter sounded panicky.

The Pyske parents whistled to their children, and the flock flew toward the barn.

Eleanor wiped her forehead. "Let's keep going, guys. It's too hot to stand here."

They continued to the end of the point and paused, deciding which way to go.

"Let's go through the park and then cut across by the lake," Rob suggested. "It's a little longer, but less road to contend with."

They rode to the far end of the field and ducked beneath the tree branches that concealed the entrance to the old logging road. As soon as they entered the woods, the temperature dropped several degrees, cooler beneath the canopy of leaves.

"How far is the swimming hole?" Willow asked.

"Not far," Rob said. "We'll follow the river and then cut below the lake. It's a sweet spot."

"So … about Doris," Eleanor said.

Jack shuddered and made a face. "What about her?"

"What do you think that was all about?"

"Who knows?" Rob said.

"Who cares?" Jack laughed.

"Aw, come on. You weren't a little bit curious?" Eleanor asked.

"What is it with girls, anyway? If I hear something about a junky old relic and someone who's looking for it, who's in a rotten mood and headed this way, my instinct is to head in the other direction. You? You're drawn like a moth to a flame. Look, El, she's a witch. A *witch*! And a nasty one at that. Did you miss the look on Camedon's face? Nope. Not interested." Jack stuck his fingers in his ears and sang, "La la la."

Eleanor ignored him. "Yeah, but I want to see it. And *who* is looking for it?"

"What relic?" Sargent asked.

"When we were on the water this morning, we met a Water Witch named Doris. She unloaded something she's been hiding on Camedon. He didn't seem happy about it," Rob explained.

"What?"

"Something called the Alabaster Chalice," Eleanor said.

"No kidding!" Willow said, excited.

Ginger's ears flicked back, listening.

"Here we go," Ringo said.

"What?" asked Jack.

Ringo snorted. "The love story of the Realm."

Willow sighed. "Newlin and Doris the Fair."

Jack blew out laughing. "Doris the *Fair*?"

"They say she was so beautiful Newlin fell in love the moment he saw her." Willow sighed again.

"Well, old Doris hasn't been keeping her beauty parlor appointments," Jack said.

"Are there any mythological Beings of the Realm *not* in Maine?" Rob asked.

"No, not really," Sargent said.

"Great," Jack said.

"Told you," Baelhar's disembodied voice echoed.

Rob pointed to a break in the trees. "Take the path ahead to the left."

"You mean the one by Camedon?" Eleanor asked.

The Keeper sat on a rock ahead and waggled his fingers at them.

"Now what?" Jack muttered.

"I heard that," the Keeper said. "Just reminding Eleanor that Gunnr will be looking for her at four o'clock."

"I didn't forget."

"How come she gets to go and we don't?" asked Jack.

"Because I'm special," Eleanor said. She turned to Camedon. "Where do I meet him?"

"He'll meet you at the house."

"Okay."

"Excellent," the Keeper said, and disappeared with a *POP*.

The horses veered off the logging road to a narrower path alongside the river. They followed it in silence, enjoying the shade and the sounds of the river. The path ended at a busy road, the lake on the other side.

Rob reined Sargent to the south. "We have to cross. Careful, it's busy."

"There's Maiden's Cliff," Flora said, looking at the sheer rock cliffs to the north. "Isn't it beautiful?"

"Um, yeah. Eilvain thought so, too." Eleanor shivered, remembering the Noctivagus threatening to throw her from the top.

They waited for a break in the traffic and crossed, keeping Flora and Willow between them. On the other side of the road, the horses passed an inlet with a natural beach.

"That's Barrett's Cove, but we're going a bit farther," Rob

told the horses. He directed them to a trail. "We'll follow this and come out by a good spot on the river. It's deep enough to swim, but calm."

It wasn't far, and they broke through the trees by a pool in the river.

"Quite satisfactory," Sargent said, looking around.

"Yes. But who's that?" Flora pointed.

Chapter Five

A FIGURE LAY SUNNING HERSELF ON THE ROCKS SLOPING TO the water. At the sound of their voices, she sat up.

Eleanor knew immediately by her appearance and attire, she was of the Realm. The wrap she wore clung to her skin, moving fluidly with her. The layers of sheer fabric could have been wet or dry. Her silky, pale hair had the same quality. Eleanor surmised, like Doris, she was a Being of the waters, but was relieved to see legs instead of a tail.

"My lucky day! The Driscolls, if I'm not mistaken," she greeted them. "I'm Meg, Water Sprite of Megunticook."

"Meg. Of course." Jack snickered. "Why not Brooke?"

Eleanor shushed him, afraid she might hear.

She did. Her smile grew. "Meg is easier to pronounce than my real name. You're Jack. Your reputation precedes you."

"Hello, Meg. I'm Flora and this is Willow. That's Rob and Sargent, Eleanor and Ginger, and Jack is on Ringo. We came for a swim." Flora took another extraordinary occurrence of the Realm completely in stride. Rob, Jack, and Eleanor shared indulgent smiles.

"Hey. Mind if we join you?" Eleanor asked.

"Oh, please do. I was hoping I'd meet you, but I didn't think it would be so soon. I *just* saw Seaton in the Harbor." She slid into the water. "Come on. Water's nice, and the only rocks are way over there. The bottom is all sand here."

Willow and Flora walked in, Ringo and Jack right behind them. Rob held Sargent back, letting Ginger and Eleanor go first. Odd. Rob was more considerate than Jack, but that only went so far. He still hadn't spoken. He just stood on the sand with Sargent and watched Meg.

His loss. He could stand there if he wanted to, but Eleanor wasn't keeping him company. She and Ginger walked farther into the water, Ginger stepping with care. The cold water hit Eleanor's toes and felt wonderful. The deeper Ginger went, the farther up Eleanor's leg the water rose. Soon it covered Ginger's back, and the horse sighed with pleasure, enjoying the reprieve from the heat.

Jack and Ringo were in deeper water. Ringo swam with Jack beside him holding his mane.

Meg swam closer to Eleanor and floated on her back. She stuck her toes in the air, examining them. "I'm so glad you showed up today. I've been wondering about something for a while. I've seen paint on ladies' toes, here in the lake …"

Eleanor smiled. "It's called toenail polish."

"And where does one find … toenail polish?" Meg asked.

"Usually at a drug store. I could bring you some."

"Oh, would you? What color do you think would look best? Something shocking? That shows in the water? Orange? Maybe a bright pink. I want it to show downstream." Her giggle rippled over the water like a fountain.

Eleanor liked her. The Sprite was fun. She appeared a few years older than Eleanor, but in the Realm, who knew? Life spans were different among Beings of the Realm.

Eleanor turned and asked Rob, "Are you coming in or what?"

"Yeah. In a minute."

The Sprite dove and surfaced next to Jack. "Race you," she

said, and started for the other side of the river.

Jack followed in steady strokes, but Meg cavorted around him, laughing. She flipped and rolled, performing acrobatic moves like a porpoise.

Without warning, she dove ahead of Jack, reared out of the water and threw her arms wide, obstructing his path as a triangular head broke the surface.

It was that of a Dragon, with horns decorating its thick brow, and heavily lidded eyes. As its serpentine body rose from the depths, wing-like fins on its sides surfaced.

Jack froze, and Ringo backed toward Willow and Flora. Rob leapt from Sargent's back and ran into the water.

Baelhar and two Elves materialized above Jack, swords drawn.

Meg kept her hands in the air, shielding Jack from the Dragon. She waved one behind her, indicating everyone should be still. "What brings you inland, Mighty Nob?" she asked the beast.

"The seas are unsettled," it said. "Strife comes this way." When it spoke, the words rolled together in a deep rumble.

"You can't stay in the river," she said. "You'll be seen."

"I cannot stay in the bay. Who is it you shield?" He stretched his neck trying to see beyond her.

Jack tensed, but stayed still.

"Humans who are *aware*. Camedon won't thank you for hurting them, or any others."

The Dragon snorted. "I don't eat Humans. Nasty things."

"I didn't say *eat*. I said *hurt*." Her lips curled into a knowing smile and she tilted her head to one side. "Don't play your word games with me, Sea Dragon. I know your ways."

"Are you aware, young Sprite, the Alabaster Chalice has risen from the depths and is unguarded? In the hands of land dwellers?"

It was that of a Dragon, with horns decorating its thick brow, and heavily lidded eyes.

"Yes. It will be returned to Newlin."

"The Undine Prince failed to protect the artifact. Perhaps he's forfeited the honor bestowed upon the Undine to guard the artifact." The great beast blinked his yellow eyes slowly, studying the Sprite.

Meg assessed him, brow raised. "What do you know?"

"Who said I know anything?"

"Stop playing games, Nob. You ventured two miles inland in fresh water, something you find entirely distasteful. You would never do such a thing unless you were hiding or fleeing. From what does Nob, the Great Midgard Serpent, Sea Dragon of Penobscot Bay, hide. Flee. One wonders."

"There are those who seek to reunite the Elements," the Dragon said. "The Chalice's Magyk is a beacon and will attract those who would misuse it."

"But why would you care? The Chalice is not your concern. What is your interest in this? What have you done?" Meg studied him suspiciously.

The dragon cocked his head at an arrogant angle. "I have no idea what you are talking about."

His act didn't fool Meg. "Save your bluster. You're welcome to stay, but know this. We must cohabitate with the Humans, and these waters have rules you must observe. You will avoid any and all contact. You mustn't even be seen. Do I make myself clear?"

"You have no lordship over me," Nob dismissed the Sprite. A fan of thin, ribbed skin expanded behind his horns in a crowning ruff of displeasure. It reminded Eleanor of a Siamese fighting fish, or a peacock, and a nervous laugh bubbled up. She swallowed it.

Meg rose farther out of the water. "Oh, yes. Yes I do, here. You will not risk the peaceful balance we've maintained for so long. Our fresh water world is much smaller and more vulnerable than your world is, and you will not disrupt it. You will *not* bring to our waters that from which you flee. Sanctuary is granted, but it has a price. Do you understand?"

"Yes," he said, grudgingly.

"Excellent. I will let the others know of your presence and you won't be disturbed."

Nob disappeared into the depths without answering her. A ripple on the water's surface moved downstream in his underwater wake. Meg watched it for several moments, and then turned to the others.

"You'll have no problems from him," she assured them. "His bark is worse than his bite. Always has been. Furthermore, he's worried … although of what, I know not." She noticed Jack's face and smiled. "You're fine, Jack." She put her arm under his and swam him to Ringo.

Jack was ashen. "I don't think I'm fine. What *was* that thing?" He shivered. "I'm never going swimming again." He put his arm over Ringo's back and hung there, his forehead on the horse's withers.

Baelhar and the Elves settled on the riverbank. "That was Nob. The Sea Dragon of Penobscot Bay—and a bit beyond— but Penobscot Bay is homeport. Dragons are territorial, even Sea Dragons. You're right, Meg. He's up to something. Freshwater's considered slumming to those of the sea. He wouldn't be here unless he was hiding," he said.

"I don't think I want to see what *he's* hiding from," Eleanor said.

"He's worried. He's either done something, or he's feeling guilty. Maybe because he knew Doris had the Alabaster Chalice and didn't say anything, but I don't think so. Something strange is going on." Meg was distracted, and different than the gay, playful Sprite they'd first met. "I need to go. You needn't worry. Nob won't bother you again. For all his bluffing he well knows the ramifications of being seen in the river or the lake."

Chapter Six

"Did Camedon give you my message?"

Eleanor started at Gunnr's voice in her head. She still wasn't comfortable speaking in the way of the Elves. When Eleanor tensed, Ginger flicked her ears back. Eleanor gave her withers a pat of reassurance.

"We're almost home. We went swimming, but we're coming down the point road now. Where are you?" she asked.

"Standing in the barn. With your Hob."

Eleanor smiled, visualizing that.

"We've met all sorts of Beings today."

"I bet. The word's out."

"Everyone keeps saying that."

"Humans new to the Realm are a big deal, but with the recent excitement, curiosity about you is even higher."

"Eilvain?"

"Yes, and Gladstone, too. A disgraced Keeper ... nothing like that has ever happened. And here you are." Gunnr waved as they rounded the last bend on the point road.

They walked through the stone pillars flanking the driveway. Once through, the drive split and the horses headed toward the barn. Hala and Mack heard them and trotted over to the fence. The kids dismounted as the Hob, Floyd, hurried out the barn doors to meet them, Gunnr following behind. He leaned against one of the doors watching Floyd hustle about.

"Hi Gunnr," Flora said. "Meet my pony, Willow." She led Willow over to the Night Elf.

"Hello, Willow." Gunnr stroked the pony's nose so she could smell him. "And if I'm not mistaken, we have Ringo, Sargent, and Ginger."

"How'd you know that?" asked Jack.

"Floyd told me," Gunnr said, bemused.

The kids removed the horses' bridles and Floyd opened the pasture gate. As soon as Ringo was back in the pasture he found a bare spot and rolled, sending dust into the air. Everyone moved into the barn.

Jack turned to Gunnr. "So how come El gets to go with you and the rest of us don't?"

"I'm starting with Eleanor, but eventually you'll join us. Camedon has questions about Eleanor's ability to speak in the way of the Elves, and he wants to see what her capabilities are. Then we'll see if you share them. Humans have never done this, but no one's ever tried, either. Language is the gift of Humans, so he thinks with some training, you can communicate in the Elven way also, without the help of the pendants."

An awful thought occurred to Eleanor. "Can all Elves hear us when we speak?"

"Only if you want them to," Gunnr assured her. "We have a private connection. Think of it in terms of roads—we have a private direct road no one else can travel on, but we can also take the highway with all the other cars. Speaking in the way of the Elves is much like that. We can converse privately with one another if we have the right mental path, or all at once."

"How does one *find* the right mental path?" Rob asked.

"It's almost automatic if you know one another and easier the better you know them. You reach for someone and you find them because you *know* them." He paused, searching for the right words. "Similar to envisioning someone in your head, or imagining the sound of their voice."

"Hey, speaking of Camedon, have you seen him today?" asked Jack.

"Talked to him earlier."

"Did he tell you what Doris the Horrid gave him?"

Gunnr smiled at Jack's description of the witch. "Yes, he told me about the Alabaster Chalice."

"There's more. When we went swimming we met a Water Sprite."

"Where?"

"Beside the dam, in the river. Her name's Meg, and she's pretty cool. When the Sea Dragon showed up, she gave him a lecture about being seen. He took off in a huff," Jack said.

"Sea Dragon? What Sea Dragon?"

"Nob." Jack shuddered.

"Nob was inland? In fresh water?" Gunnr frowned. "I bet Meg gave him a lecture. Sprites are protective of their waters."

"She did. She was ... something," Rob said, more to himself.

Jack caught Eleanor's eye and smirked.

So he'd noticed Rob's odd behavior around the Sprite too. Huh.

"Almost ready?" Gunnr asked Eleanor.

"Yes. Where're we going?"

"Just to my home, today. We'll go through the passage in the cavern."

"I'm all set. See you, guys."

Eleanor and Gunnr left, walked past the house and down the steps to the beach. Gunnr took a deep breath and looked out over the water. The smell of the salt water permeated the still afternoon air.

"It's hot," Eleanor said, lifting her hair off her neck.

"Use your mind."

"Why?"

Gunnr didn't answer her.

Eleanor sighed, but reached for him in her mind. *"Fine. Why?"*

"Practice. I want you to exercise the ability to reach out with your mind."

"Why?" Eleanor repeated. She still wasn't entirely sure why Camedon wanted her to work with Gunnr.

"Camedon suspects you have strengths we've not realized. Strengths uncommon to most Humans."

"Flora's the one you should be working with. She was immediately comfortable with her awakened senses."

"Typical of her age, but I didn't have the immediate connection with Flora I did with you."

They walked toward the cavern and Eleanor considered his words.

"But I didn't connect with Queen Solvanha, or any other Elves. Maybe it's because of the pendant you made. Or maybe it's you."

"I don't think so. You have an innate empathy."

"I don't know what you mean."

"Sympathy is understanding how someone feels. Empathy is feeling that feeling. You're receptive to emotions surrounding you. You absorb them. I suspect you even affect the feelings of others. I noticed it when we first met, and I noticed it after the battle with Eilvain, too, but I dismissed it to the experience. I noticed it again, however, in the Lee with Camedon and Gladstone. Tensions were high and you were affected by them."

"Because I spoke up?" Eleanor frowned.

"Do you often confront an entire group of strangers?"

Eleanor thought for a moment. "No."

"I thought not."

"I was angry. Gladstone was lying."

"Yes, he was, but I suspect you would not have done so if you'd only been experiencing your own anger. You absorbed all the other tensions in the room, and the barrage of feelings compelled you to act. Your reaction to those situations, coupled with the immediate connection we shared, made me wonder if you have stronger gifts than most Humans. Camedon and Charlotte agree."

"You discussed this? You discussed me?" Eleanor wasn't sure if that annoyed her or not.

"Yes. Your parents, too," Gunnr said. "Our history is long, Eleanor. Even after Humans left the Realm, Elves and Humans continued to interact over the centuries. There's only been one other Human with the ability to speak in the way of the Elves. Ever. Only one who possessed the innate ability to connect in the way we connected."

They had reached the cavern's entrance.

"That you know of," Eleanor pointed out.

"Still. Your ability is like hers, and it's rare. Virtually unheard of."

"Hers? Who are you talking about?"

Gunnr faced Eleanor, a strange look on his face. "A woman who drank from the Alabaster Chalice. My Mother."

Chapter Seven

"Your mother?" Eleanor asked out loud.

Eleanor followed Gunnr into the cavern. "Hold on. Your *mother* was Human?"

"Yes. She was born Human. Speak with your mind."

"So she became an Elf?"

"Yes … no … in a manner of speaking. Long story."

"Wasn't your father the Elven King?"

"Yes," Gunnr said.

"So you're half Elven? Half Human?"

"Technically, yes, though Elven genetics are stronger than Human genetics. On the rare occasions offspring are born of such a union, Elven genetics are dominant."

"So maybe it's you and not me who's different."

"It's possible, of course, but I don't think so. With no training, no practice, your mind was open. You weren't even aware of it, but I was able to read your mind simply by standing next to you. You're young and untrained, but that you connected to me and merged your mind so completely that we even feel each other's emotions shows us how powerful you may be. And, also how vulnerable you are," Gunnr said.

Reaching the rear of the cavern, he paused and faced her. "You have uncommon gifts, and we need to test the limits of those gifts. We need to know what you're capable of, and we need to teach you to protect yourself."

"Protect from what?"

"Protect you from inadvertently connecting with anyone else. Or any*thing* else."

Eleanor shuddered, imagining Eilvain in her mind. She'd do whatever it took to protect herself from being vulnerable to a monster like that again. "What do I do?"

"Merge your mind with me. Picture me in your mind, reach out to me."

"Now?"

"Yes, now. I want to try something."

"Okay. Now what?"

"Reach into my mind. See what I see."

"I don't know what you mean."

"Remember in the cave when I saw through your eyes? Merge your mind with mine. Your being. Your whole self, and then see what I see."

Eleanor concentrated. Nothing happened. She scrunched her eyes and concentrated harder. She focused, pushing her self into Gunnr's mind.

Nothing.

"I don't know what you want me to do." Eleanor ran her hand through her hair, frustrated.

"You're trying too hard. Just relax and talk to me, but … closer. Expand your presence in my head, and allow mine into yours. Imagine our minds superimposed over one another. Don't force it, allow it."

Eleanor made herself relax and sought outside herself. She pictured a connection flowing between them. She reached for him and his sight wholly, and caught a quick glimpse of something—the wall of the cavern—before she lost it.

"Again. Keep it easy," Gunnr encouraged her. "Don't just

picture it. Be it."

She opened herself fully to the connection between them, let it wash over her. Take her with it. She, it, and he *were*.

The image flashed again in her mind. It was the wall of the cavern, but covered with an intricate pattern of silver. She physically turned to look at the wall and lost the image.

"It's okay. You were doing it. Use your mind, not your body. Separate physical from mental."

"What's on the wall?"

"Woven protections placed on the passage to prevent those who should not use it from doing so."

"Why can't I see it? With my eyes?"

"Humans can't see protections because they don't use magic. They can't weave them, so they only see the rock in the physical dimension. Let's try it again."

Eleanor shook the tension out of her shoulders, took a deep breath, and closed her eyes. She reached out, touched his mind lightly, and then merged herself completely with him.

The connection was complete, and she saw, heard, and felt everything Gunnr did. She focused on the images, stabilizing them in her own mind. Once she did, she was able to examine the image.

The intricate protections on the rock face fascinated her. She studied them for several minutes.

"You're doing it. And you aren't just seeing, you're looking. Excellent."

"What are they? Is it language? I can't read it."

"No, not language. Energy. Magic is handling energy. Arranging, manipulating, finessing."

"The protections are beautiful."

"Each person weaves their own. These are Camedon's,

*though the ones he uses here are familiar to many of us. I can
remove them, and replace them."*

"If I see them, can I remove them?"

"That is the question, isn't it? I'm wondering. Perhaps, with
practice. You have a healer's heart. Healing, or Heila, as the Elves
practice, is also handling energy." Gunnr raised his hands, and
moved them in a series of fluid motions, unraveling the protective silver threads on the passage wall. The strands curled into
a ball at his feet.

Eleanor was torn between watching him, with her own eyes,
and watching the protections unravel, with his. She chose the
protections, and opened her mind, this time with relative ease,
sharing his vision.

"You missed one."

"Show off."

"I'm practicing."

"You're a quick study. Good, because there's more."

"Today?" Eleanor asked. She was already brain weary.

He smiled. "No. Today we're going to do something else.
Baelhar and Sehlis have offered to help. It's time to see if you can
find the mental path to speak with others in the way of the Elves."

"No. I'm not ready for that."

"Yes, you are."

Eleanor frowned. "I don't want to be in anyone else's mind.
I don't want them in mine."

"Why?"

"I just don't. It's ... it's ..."

*"I know this is new to you, but we need to teach you to use
your skills. To build your defenses. And we should establish your
communication path with Baelhar as he's head of the guard
Solvanha assigned to you."*

"Why can't you teach me to use the common mental path Elves use?"

"It's not safe. The Noctivagi who were Elves can also hear the common path."

"Do you think there are more? Here?"

"We don't know that there aren't. Ever."

"I still don't like this."

"It'll be fine. You'll see."

Eleanor wrinkled her nose. Easy for him to say. He wouldn't be the one looking like a fool in front of an audience.

His smile flashed in her mind's eye. "You won't have an audience, and you're not going to look like a fool."

"Stop reading my mind! That's the problem."

"You speak easily with me."

"You're different."

"No, I'm not. You may not even be able to connect with the others, but I suspect you will, and you'll master it as quickly as you mastered seeing through my eyes. It's only another way to communicate, Eleanor. That's all."

Eleanor considered his point for a moment, and then said, "I'll do it on one condition."

"What's that?"

"You teach me how to defend myself."

"Teaching you to speak in the way of the Elves is a defense."

"You know what I mean. Physically."

"All right," he agreed. "We'll teach you some ways to defend yourself. Physically."

He took her hand and stepped through the rock face. It felt thick for a moment, but Eleanor was becoming accustomed to the feeling of passages.

They emerged in one of the pillared tunnels ringing the stone rotunda that was the center of Gunnr's home.

"I think you should explain to me how to tell the tunnels apart. How to get out of here," Eleanor said. "You know. Like in case of a fire."

He chuckled. "You cannot gain entry to my home, or leave, without removing the safeguards," he said.

"You're kidding."

"No. Not all in the Realm welcome my presence."

Eleanor made a face. It was humiliating to be escorted here, as if she were a small child again, holding her mother's hand to cross the street.

"What's the matter?"

"It's hard to be part of a world, but not have any of the abilities the other Beings in that world have," Eleanor said.

"That's exactly the reason we're here. Why I want you to work with Baelhar and Sehlis. To help you acquire some of those skills. Use your mind to speak."

"Can you at least show me how to tell the difference between tunnels?"

"In the Nave? The numbers on the pediments might help."

Eleanor examined the tops of one of the tunnels ringing the stone chamber. "I don't see any numbers."

"They're Runic. Ahhh. You had to touch the Rune Stone before you could read it, didn't you? Interesting. It's carved," Gunnr mused.

Eleanor wasn't prepared when he lifted her and she let out a little gasp. They floated upward until they were level with a pediment. Eleanor touched the stone with her finger and the intricate carving became a word.

"Four."

"Yes," he answered, pleased.

"Did you build this? All of this?"

"With magic, yes. Can you read the others?"

Eleanor looked around. "One, two, three, five. And Hic Contenta Sum is carved into the center of the platform. Here I am happy?" She asked, puzzled.

"Yes. Here I am happy," he said, looking around the Nave. "This is where I am safe and at peace."

"No place like home, Dorothy?"

Gunnr smiled.

"Did it take you long to build this?"

He shrugged. "Not really. Need is a powerful motivator."

"I don't understand."

"I needed a new home after I was exiled. A safe one."

"You can't return to Álfheimr? Ever?"

"No. I wouldn't be welcome."

"But you and Queen Solvanha made peace."

"We have, but Sol's not the only one with whom I must make peace. Many would be angered. I wouldn't put Sol in that position."

"Are your parents still alive?"

"It's another story for another day, Eleanor."

Gunnr's tone left no room for argument, so she asked, "But where do all the tunnels lead?"

"Some lead to other parts of my home. Some exit to other sides of the mountain."

"Gunnr!" Baelhar and Sehlis entered the Nave from the tunnel marked number one. Amused to see them floating by the pediment, Baelhar asked, "Hanging around?"

Gunnr drifted down and set Eleanor on the floor. He greeted Baelhar formally in the way of the Elven Warriors, grasping forearms.

"Thank you for helping with this," Gunnr said to him. He turned to Sehlis, "Both of you. Hello, Sehlis."

"Gunnr," she answered coolly, but her expression warmed when she greeted Eleanor. "Hello, Eleanor." Sehlis, in the nature of Elves, was beautiful. Her light brown hair, cut short, curled around her face.

"Hi," Eleanor said, uncertain. Sehlis' coolness to Gunnr was awkward.

"It's fine. Sehlis is wary around me, but she came."

"This will be fun, Eleanor. It will bug Jack," Baelhar said, trying to set her at ease.

She returned his smile, but she couldn't settle her nerves. *"I really don't want to do this,"* she said to Gunnr.

"I know. It'll be all right, Eleanor."

Aloud, Gunnr explained, "Eleanor appears to have stronger capabilities than most Humans, but she still isn't completely comfortable speaking in the Elven way. Sol, Camedon, her parents, and I think she should practice establishing private mental paths with individual Elves rather than the common path Elves use. It's harder, but it's possible for communication to be overheard by the Noctivagi on the common path."

"Makes sense. I'm assuming you'd prefer her abilities not be common knowledge," Sehlis said.

"It's best. I appreciate you helping with this, Sehlis. I know Sol does as well."

"Mmm," Sehlis said noncommittally. "Where are we to work? Here?" She looked around the Nave.

"No. The library." Gunnr walked to a tunnel and indicated the others follow. Eleanor had been in this tunnel before. It more resembled a wide hallway, with a brightly woven carpet runner and portraits on the walls. They passed several doors, and Gunnr paused.

Eleanor connected with him so she could watch him unravel the safeguards. She felt his approval, but he gave no outward acknowledgement. He opened the door, waved his hand to light the room, and stood aside so they could enter.

Eleanor chose an armchair close to the door. Baelhar sat on one of the sofas, and Sehlis sat with him. Gunnr sat on another sofa. He waved his hand and a fire crackled to life in the fireplace to warm the cool, subterranean dwelling.

"So, what did you have in mind?" Baelhar asked.

Chapter Eight

"ELEANOR SPEAKS EASILY TO ME IN THE ELVEN WAY. ON THE way here, we tried something else, and she was also able to share my vision. She both saw what I was seeing, and looked around, herself. Today, I'd like to see if she can find a path to Baelhar. On her own."

"I don't know how—"

"You do," Gunnr cut her off. "Lean back, close your eyes, and relax."

Eleanor started to speak but Gunnr held up his hand. "Just lean back."

Eleanor felt the push in his voice, and shoved it away, but she leaned her head back and closed her eyes.

"Resisting compulsion is good defensive practice."

"Get on with it."

"Relax for a few minutes. Listen to the fire, clear your mind." Aloud, Gunnr explained, "Eleanor first found our path of communication with a pendant I crafted, but she exhibited receptiveness before that. She is an empath, and though untrained, she's a strong one. She doesn't only absorb emotions, she affects them, too."

"Has she done this with anyone but you?" Sehlis asked.

"Yes, but I'm not sure anyone recognized it at the time. Least of all, her. She doesn't realize what she does differs from other Humans. And why would she?"

"Eleanor," Gunnr addressed her again in a quiet, encouraging voice. "I want you, when you're ready, to seek outside yourself for Baelhar. Picture him, but open your mind and let yourself reach for him. When you're ready."

Eleanor listened to the fire snap and pop. She was tempted to ignore him and take a nap.

He didn't understand. It wasn't that she didn't appreciate the help offered by the Light Elves, but she didn't want to be special. The die had been cast, though. Gunnr wouldn't let it go. There'd be no faking that she couldn't do it, either. She could do this, she knew it as well as Gunnr. And if Rob, Jack, Flora, and she were to be part of the Realm, they'd need every advantage they had.

When she and Gunnr merged minds, the connection was complete. There were no barriers and they shared thoughts freely, but with him it wasn't awkward. If she was going to do this with others, she needed filters. Control. Eleanor remembered what Gunnr had said about handling energy, and something clicked. She remembered the Elves disappearing in a shaft of light, Gunnr handling a ball of light energy in his hands, and the light energy the Elves used to *heil*.

Physically handling something was an image easy for her to visualize. It gave her something concrete on which to focus, to imagine controlling. She could limit what she shared to the light she handled.

She could do this, but she'd do it her way. Eleanor took a deep breath and sent herself searching for Sehlis instead of Baelhar. Eleanor conjured a shaft of light energy in her mind. Energy unique to her, a part of her. It grew stronger. She defined the edges carefully, so that she only shared what she wanted to, and what she shared was only shared with Sehlis. When it felt true, she sent it, projecting it straight to Sehlis. When she found what she sought, she allowed it to flow between them. The light connected them.

"Sehlis. Can you hear me?"

Sehlis' laughter echoed in her head. *"Not one for orders, are you? Well done, little one, well done indeed."*

Eleanor ignored the praise and asked, *"Have you known Gunnr since before the Ritual?"*

"Yes. We grew up together."

"Tell me something from then, from when you knew him."

"Hmmm—this is more of a question for Baelhar. They were inseparable when they were young. Let me think … all right. When Gunnr was a child and first learning to shapeshift, he had a hard time with it. Once, when he shifted back to his Elven form, he was missing a hand. Solvanha teased him mercilessly. She called him handsome for years."

"Eleanor?" Gunnr prodded.

Eleanor raised her hand, silencing him. "Give me a minute." Sehlis chuckled aloud.

She sat up and opened her eyes. "Did they really call you handsome when you were young?" Eleanor asked him

Gunnr looked to Baelhar, who shook his head, denying any communication. He frowned and turned to Sehlis.

"Your student has a mind of her own," Sehlis said with a smile.

Gunnr's eyebrow went up, but Eleanor could tell he was pleased. "Now try Baelhar," he said, and then added, "Please."

"Fine." Eleanor leaned back again and closed her eyes. She felt Gunnr in a corner of her mind, observing. She drew together a ball of light energy, and focused it. Then she directed the defined beam at Baelhar. When it touched him she said, *"We don't want guards."*

She felt his smile in her mind.

"I'd hoped to repay the favor you did me by ensuring your safety while you become acclimated to the Realm. Won't you allow me the privilege?" Baelhar asked.

Eleanor grinned. *"No."*

He chuckled, and Eleanor opened her eyes. Baelhar and Gunnr stared intently at each other. Sehlis watched them, curious, and Eleanor realized they were speaking in the way of the Elves. About her.

Someone knocked on the door, interrupting the exchange between the two. Gunnr waved it open.

Camedon entered, holding Doris' crusty container, with Agnes on his shoulder. He surveyed the room and asked, "And how is our first lesson progressing?"

The Keeper entered and sat on the sofa beside Gunnr. As he passed, Agnes hopped from his shoulder to the arm of Eleanor's chair. She gave Eleanor's hand a quick peck.

"I wish you'd find a new greeting," Eleanor said to the crow, rubbing her hand.

"You won't be surprised to learn Eleanor exceeded your expectations," Gunnr informed the Keeper. "Even being inclined to be uncooperative."

Eleanor ignored him. She stroked Agnes and gazed into the fire. The benign expression on her face belied the activity in her mind. She concentrated, gathering light energy. When it felt strong enough, she focused and sent it out to Camedon like a missile.

"He's lying. I was not uncooperative."

"Good heavens!" Camedon exclaimed, jerking his head to her. "That's amazing."

Smiles grew as each of the Elves realized what Eleanor

had done. She would never admit it, but it felt good. She felt good. Strong.

"*It's supposed to feel good,*" Gunnr told her.

"*Stop reading my mind.*"

"*It was hard to shut you out before. It's almost impossible now.*"

"*Everyone can hear me?*" Eleanor asked, alarmed.

"*No. You closed the connection with the others. Snuffed the light, if you will. Your connection with me is of a different nature. You don't close it.*" Gunnr wasn't looking at her, but she felt him considering it.

"*Go away.*"

Gunnr turned his attention to Camedon, and the barnacled lump. "Is that it? The Chalice?"

"Yes. I need something to open it."

Gunner removed a dagger from a sheath on his belt and handed it to Camedon.

Camedon examined the lump's sides, and inserted the dagger into a seam. He began to pry, and everyone in the room sat forward to see. Intent on protecting its secrets, the container resisted his efforts. He put it between his knees so he could use both hands, and wrenched several times. Still, nothing loosened.

Gunnr moved closer and held his hands out. "Let me try."

Camedon handed him the container and the dagger. Gunnr twisted the container in every direction, tapping the dagger's handle along the edges. He then slid the dagger's blade into another seam, pried, and the wood creaked. Camedon pointed to another edge along the top, and Gunnr slid the dagger in. Barnacle fragments littered the table, sofa, and floor. With pressure on the opposing seam, the container's lid popped off and fell to the floor.

Gunnr set it on the table, and everyone drew closer.

Eleanor inspected the piece Gunnr had removed. The inside of the container was free from the ravages of the sea. Decorative bands of iron reinforced the wood.

Gunnr looked at Camedon. "Would you like the honors?"

"No, go ahead."

Gunnr pulled a large bundle from the container and set it on the table. Carefully, he unwrapped layers of wet cloth.

As he pulled last layer away, he frowned, as did Baelhar, Sehlis, and Camedon. Before them sat a wet pile of assorted items, but no Chalice.

Chapter Nine

"I DON'T UNDERSTAND," SEHLIS SAID.

Camedon stared at the pile, eyebrows halfway to his hairline.

"Was Doris mistaken? Lying?" Agnes asked.

Camedon stood, walked to the fireplace, and stared at the flames for a few moments before answering. He turned and said, "I wouldn't have guessed it, but she could have handed me a red herring." He frowned. "Her worry seemed genuine, though. She was desperate to get rid of the Chalice. Adamant."

"Doris is a slippery old thing," Baelhar reminded him, and then added, "No pun intended."

Camedon frowned. "She is, but it rang sincere. I suppose I have to find her. You'll excuse me?" He sighed, steeling himself for the encounter with the Water Witch.

"Shall I keep this stuff here?" Gunnr asked.

"If you wouldn't mind, I'd appreciate it. I'll collect it later. Care to join me, Agnes?" Camedon moved toward the door, and the crow flew to his shoulder. "Wish us luck." With a final look at those in the room and the wet debris, he left.

Intrigued by the pile, Eleanor knelt beside the table. "What're these? There's one in the hidey-hole in the barn." She pointed to several thin, oval items with a fluid iridescent quality to them, much like oil on water.

Gunnr picked one up. "Sea Dragon scales."

"Like Nob!" Eleanor said, realizing the Dragon was the same odd golden color.

"Yes," Gunnr nodded.

"This pile is someone's collection. Look at all the sea glass."

"That isn't sea glass, but you're right," Baelhar said. "This *is* someone's collection. And if we can figure out whose, it might point us in the direction of the Chalice."

Gunnr and Sehlis nodded.

"What do you mean, this isn't sea glass?" Eleanor asked. She chose a pale blue piece, rubbing her thumb over the worn surface.

"Those are shedder scales from the tail of a Water Witch," Gunnr explained. He wrinkled his nose in distaste. "They harden to glass after they're shed."

An image of Doris popped into Eleanor's mind, and she dropped the piece back on the pile. She thought of the jar of beach glass in her room. Might as well have been a jar of old fingernail clippings.

She wiped her hands on her pants, picked up Gunnr's dagger and used the blade to push around the pile. It appeared mostly junk: rocks, rusted hardware, a length of chain, a few shells. Something caught the light. A fat gray pearl with an irregular surface. Still, nothing revealing.

Sehlis stood. "Are we done?"

Baelhar also rose. "I think so."

Eleanor was relieved. She was tired and wanted to go home.

Gunnr joined them at the door. "I'll see you out. Back in a minute, Eleanor."

She gave the Elves a wave and moved to the sofa. Pulling her feet under her and leaning back, she looked around the room. Bookshelves lined every wall but one, which displayed a row of portraits. She'd noticed them the first time she'd been here, and they'd intrigued her. The paintings were richly detailed, and Eleanor had only ever seen anything comparable in museums. Surrounding each subject were many smaller scenes of places, Beings, and happenings in the Realm. Each unique, Eleanor surmised, to the Elf in the portrait. One was of Queen Solvanha, and Eleanor figured the others were also members of Gunnr's family. The first portrayed a man wearing a crown similar to Queen Solvanha's, and with the same dark blue eyes as Gunnr and Queen Solvanha. Their father, the Elven King? She wondered which was his mother and guessed it was the woman in the second painting. Eleanor studied the portrait. There was something familiar about her. As she pondered who the woman reminded her of, she sensed, rather than heard, Gunnr's return.

"We have one last thing to do today."

"I'm done. I'm tired and hungry and I want to go home."

"I think you'll like this. I have someone I want you to meet. Come with me." Gunnr didn't wait for her to agree, but left the room.

She followed him to the cavernous rotunda. Gunnr led her toward an ugly statue squatting on a platform, but as Eleanor moved closer it looked less stone-like, and more leathery. It didn't move, but somehow Eleanor realized that it wasn't a statue at all—the thing was *alive*. She stopped, dead in her tracks.

Hunched, it was approximately four feet tall, and looked powerful. A square snout shaped its bony face. Eleanor was relieved its eyes were closed, and hoped it wouldn't open them. Warty horn nubs poked from the crest of its heavy brow, and thick talons curled on its feet.

Gunnr gestured her closer.

Eleanor took a step back, and whispered, "What is it?"

"*She*. This is Motte. She's a Gargoyle. She found me, took up residence, and assumed guardianship of my home. It's the nature of Gargoyles. With Motte here you needn't worry about the protections. She will allow you in or out as you please."

A square snout shaped its bony face.

Eleanor looked at Gunnr as if he were crazy. She wasn't getting anywhere near that thing.

"I know you're not asleep, Motte," Gunnr said.

One black eye opened, took in Eleanor, then Gunnr, and closed again. "What is it?" she croaked. Her voice was rough, and Eleanor knew she rarely used it.

"I'd like you to meet someone."

"I know who she is." The Gargoyle sounded bored.

"But she doesn't know you. Open your eyes, please."

"You needn't have disturbed my slumber. She doesn't need to know me. I will know when she approaches."

"I need to know you and Eleanor can communicate."

"If her brain functions, we can communicate. Should there be a need. I don't foresee a need." She still refused to open her eyes.

Eleanor agreed. She didn't foresee a need, either. "Maybe another time?" Eleanor urged Gunnr. The creature petrified her. There was no way she'd disturb this thing.

"Very well," Gunnr said.

The Gargoyle spread her wings with a sharp slap. When she lifted from the pedestal, Eleanor flinched. Motte flew to a pediment, settled into a crouch, and stilled. For a moment she appeared to be a statue, and then she faded until she was the color of the surrounding stone. Only a vague outline was discernible.

"Can we go? Now?" Eleanor whispered, moving toward the tunnel marked with the Runic 'two'.

With a displeased look at the Gargoyle, he followed.

"She won't hurt you."

"You've got that right. I don't plan on ever getting near her again."

Gunnr removed the woven protections at the tunnel's end,

took Eleanor's hand, and led her through the rock face. They exited in the cavern on the beach.

"What time is it?"

"Use your mind," he reminded her.

"No. I've used it enough today. I'm tired."

"And overwhelmed. I'm sorry Motte frightened you. I thought you'd be happy to know you weren't limited by your lack of magic."

"I am. Thrilled. Can we go?"

His smile reached his eyes. So few of his smiles did, and it deflated her prickliness.

"I'm just tired. And hungry. I've missed dinner, haven't I?" Eleanor said, seeing the darkening sky through the opening in the ledges.

Gunnr held out his hand, and a pear materialized. "Come. I'll walk you to the house."

They walked the beach's length without conversation. Eleanor ate her pear, and tossed the core into the clump of beach roses.

"You must have been hungry. You inhaled that."

"It was delicious."

"I would hope so." He wiggled his fingers and sparkles fell from them, making her laugh.

"We don't, however, need to litter," a disapproving voice came from the shadows. Floyd stepped from the rose bush, tsking, and holding the core in his hand.

"It's a core, Floyd. Mum would call it compost."

"Then it belongs in the compost pile, doesn't it? No matter, Miss. Happy to deliver this to the cellar-dweller. He can dispose of it properly." Then muttered, "If he's sober."

Ralph the Goblin sat up in a flower bed on the other side of the steps. "What do you mean, *if'n I'm sober*?" He rubbed his eyes and peered into the shadows. "Steamin' Sylph Spit! What are *you* doing here?"

Floyd was momentarily taken aback, but he recovered quickly. "I'm here to take this property in hand. Someone obviously needs to."

Ralph hopped up and shoved his flask into his waistband. "O'er my dead body. Innerfearin' Hobs! I don't care if we're kin or not, if you think you're gunna saunter in here and start bossing us all around, well, you gotta 'nother thing comin', buster."

Floyd gave Ralph a cool appraisal. "You just worry about your personal hygiene—"

The Goblin sputtered, but Floyd stepped back into the shadows, holding the offending core in front of him with two fingers.

Ralph tugged his cap farther down and marched after him.

"Patters may have been right," Eleanor murmured.

Gunnr smiled.

Five Elves took shape at the top of the steps, blocking their ascent and startling a gasp from Eleanor.

Chapter Ten

Baelhar stepped forward. "There's been another attack."

"Who?" Gunnr asked.

Baelhar glanced at Eleanor, and said to Gunnr, "You better come with us."

The two stared at each other, and Eleanor realized they were purposely communicating in the way of the Elves so as not to speak in front of her.

"Who?" Eleanor asked. Neither answered her. She reached out, grabbing Gunnr's forearm, and gasped at the image in his mind. Bloody bodies littered the ground, mutilated beyond recognition.

Gunnr gently removed her hand. The image disappeared as if a light had been shut off. He'd closed his mind to her. "Go inside, Eleanor. I need to go with Baelhar."

"Take me."

"No. Not tonight."

"I won't be in the way."

"Gunnr, take her or leave her, but we need to go. Now," Baelhar said.

Take her or leave her? Like a hat? What was that?

Gunnr saw the expression on her face. He didn't wait for her reply. "No, I'm sorry, Eleanor. Go inside." His shape blurred, and he vanished.

He was gone, the Elven Guard as well, leaving Eleanor on the steps unsure of what to do. She climbed the last three steps, crossed the terrace, and entered the dining room through the French doors.

Her mother and Rob were clearing the table.

"Oh, good," her mother said. "You're back. I saved some dinner for you. I'll heat it. Sit." She took the last glass from the table and left the room.

Rob looked at Eleanor's face and asked, "What's the matter?"

"The Elven Guard met Gunnr on the steps. There's been another attack. By Noctivagi," Eleanor told him, sinking into a chair.

"Where? Who?"

Eleanor frowned. "I don't know. They wouldn't tell me, and Gunnr wouldn't take me."

Rob looked at her as if she were nuts. "Why would you *want* to go?"

"I don't know. I can't explain it—I felt as if I should. Something's going on. They wouldn't tell me who they attacked."

"Whatever you do, don't tell Mum and Dad. They told us at dinner they're going away. Dad has a conference and Mum's going with him. Mrs. Bradford is staying with us. If you tell them there's been another attack, that there's Noctivagi in the area, they'll cancel their trip."

"I won't tell them," she said. "But someone else may."

Eleanor and Rob heard the kitchen door creak and footsteps in the hall. Their mother entered with a plate, silverware, and a glass of milk.

"Here we are," she said, setting a place at a clean spot on the table.

"Spaghetti. My favorite," she told her mother. The red sauce reminded her of the image in Gunnr's head. She pushed the image away. She felt like pushing the plate away.

"I thought you might be hungry. How was your lesson? You were gone a long time."

Eleanor took a small bite and chewed. For some reason she wasn't ready to share the details. She swallowed and said, "Good. It was hard, but I think it went okay."

"You don't have to do this, Eleanor," her mother said. "If you'd rather not, I hope you'd say so. You mustn't feel as if you have to."

"No, it's fine, Mum. It was kinda fun, and everyone's nice. Really."

"But if you change your mind—"

"I'll tell you," Eleanor assured her mother.

"I've decided to join your father on his trip. We're leaving tomorrow afternoon. I know it's short notice …" Her mother sounded uncertain.

"Rob just told me. We'll be good. You should go."

"Maybe I should speak to Charlotte," her mother said, more to herself.

"No, really, Mum. We'll be fine. Mrs. Bradford will be here, Nickerson, and …" Eleanor rolled her eyes at Rob. "An entire Elven Guard."

"If you're sure."

"We're fine. Really. Go."

"Told you," Rob said to his mother.

"Well, I guess that's that. It *has* been a long time since your father and I got away."

"I can't remember the last time," Eleanor said.

"I think the last time was your father's Aunt Millie's funeral, and that trip was only overnight."

"Where are you going?"

"San Antonio."

"Texas?"

"Yes. For a week. Are you kids sure you'll be all right?"

"Yes, Mum!"

"Okay, okay. You didn't eat much, Eleanor. Wasn't it warm enough?"

"It was good, Mum. I'm full. Thanks."

Her mother looked skeptical, but took her plate and the last few dishes and headed to the hall. "I'll be in the kitchen if you need anything."

"'Kay," Rob said.

She and Rob listened for the creak of the swinging kitchen door before they resumed their conversation.

"How *did* it really go today? Really?"

"Was I that obvious?"

"No."

"Where's everyone else?"

"Jack and Flora are watching TV in the library, and Dad's finishing his speech for the conference in his study."

"It was way bizarre, Rob. You know I can talk to Gunnr. In the way of the Elves? Without the pendant?"

"Yeah. I guess."

"Well, I can talk to all of them. It's different than with him, but I can do it—Camedon, too."

Rob frowned. "But Camedon isn't an Elf."

"No, but maybe Keepers have … like…*all* the gifts of the different Beings. Remember how he disappeared the day we found Baelhar? With the other Elves? Into the shaft of sunlight?"

"Yeah, I guess so. Huh."

"Anyway, he showed up with the container Doris made him

take, but the Chalice wasn't in it. It was just a bunch of junk."

"So, where *is* the Chalice?"

"No one knows."

"What else did you do?"

"Gunnr taught me how to see through *his* eyes. Like how he found me the night Eilvain took me?" At Rob's look of astonishment, Eleanor said, "Yeah. Like that. I could see things Humans can't, like the protections on the cavern wall."

"Are you serious? How cool is that?"

"It's kinda strange, actually," she said. She didn't really want to talk about it yet. Before he could ask any more questions, she said, "And guess what else. He has a Gargoyle."

"Who?"

"Gunnr."

"A Gargoyle? For real?"

"Yeah. She makes Doris look like Suzie Sunshine."

Rob shuddered at the mention of Doris. "She? What's her name?"

Eleanor grinned. "Motte."

"Geez, El. I want to go next time."

"Be my guest."

"But you don't know who the Noctivagi attacked?"

"No. I got a glimpse when I touched Gunnr's arm, but then he closed his mind to me. I couldn't tell. Whoever it was, they were a mess."

"Try it again," Rob urged her.

"Here? Now?"

"We'll go upstairs. Come on. Back stairs."

"We better go to your room. Flora could come into mine."

She and Rob paused at the doorway and peered into the hall. No one was about. Eleanor could hear the TV in the library and the clamor of dishes from the kitchen. They ran up the back stairs, paused to check the hall was empty, and made a break for Rob's room. Rob closed the door.

Eleanor flopped on one of the beds.

Rob sat on the edge of his. "So how do you do it?"

"Give me a minute."

"Sorry."

"No—it's fine. Just give me a minute."

She wasn't sure if she'd find Gunnr's mind still closed to her—she wasn't even certain she'd find *him*. She had no idea where he was. Eleanor gathered her thoughts, picturing him. Saw his face in her mind. The way he leaned against the wall. She let the images of him build, focused, and sent herself to him.

"Can you hear me?"

"Are you home? Is everything all right?"

"Yes. What's happening? Where are you?" Eleanor tried to see what he was seeing, but he turned toward the woods when he realized what she was doing.

"In the park. Destroying the evidence of the attack."

"Who was it?"

"Campers. No one from around here. They were just …camping." He was weary and discouraged, and his sorrow swamped her.

"Why wouldn't you take me with you?" she asked.

"Because it was a slaughter. It was a message, and a bloody one." Disgust filled his voice. *"No one should see anything like this. Least of all you."*

Eleanor bristled. *"Least of all me?"*

She expected a comment about her age, but his gentle explanation caught her off guard. *"Because you absorb emotion. The emotions of the ones here would have been too much. You've* opened your mind, but you haven't built up your defenses."

"Oh."

"We need to finish here. We'll be a while. Rest for tomorrow."

Eleanor recognized the compulsion. "Stop using your dumb voice on me."

"Don't leave the house tonight, Eleanor. Go to sleep. We'll figure it out tomorrow."

He snuffed the connection, and was gone.

She sat up and looked at Rob.

"Well?" he asked.

"No one we know. Campers in the state park, but he said it was a mess."

"How many?"

"I don't know. More than one. He said they."

"Man, El. How often does this happen and Humans are unaware?"

Eleanor didn't have an answer.

Chapter Eleven

ELEANOR STOOD FROZEN IN THE RING OF LAMP LIGHT, HER heart pounded, and she peered into the darkness.

Hatred swamped her, surrounding her so completely it masked the direction of its origin. Something malevolent watched, biding its time. Somewhere in the darkness, veiled by the shadows, it stalked her. Assessing her coldly, contemptuous of its prey.

The old ones in the area discussed it in low tones. Children whispered about it at night, frightening each other. Some said it devoured flesh. Some said it consumed souls. All were wrong.

It wasn't too late to return to the safety of the house, but she knew the house was only a temporary refuge. Sooner or later, she'd have to venture into the night. It knew this and waited. It had time on its side, and she did not. Still, terror locked her hand around the doorknob.

The night aligned itself with the monster. The wind grew stronger, masking the noise of the unnatural with the sounds of nature. Moonlight and clouds played tricks on her, moving shadows before she could see if they held any substance.

She contemplated the barn. A chasm of vulnerability stretched between her and it. She sidled out of the light, pressing her back to the wall of the house so hard the edges of the shingles dug into her skin. Edging along slowly, listening, her eyes strained in the darkness for any indication she should reverse direction and flee back.

She crouched into the shadow of a bush and took a deep breath, ready to bolt, when a hand grabbed her shoulder. Fingers dug painfully, stopping her, and her heart almost exploded. She struggled, but the hand easily restrained her. She forced herself to look up into a shadowed face.

"Watch!" he hissed.

Eleanor's eyes snapped open. Heart pounding, she lay in the darkness, afraid to move, telling herself it was only a dream. She was safe. Nothing was after her, and there was nothing in her room.

Something crashed to the floor.

Something *was* in her room.

Certain it could hear her heart pounding, she slid her hand toward the light, inch by inch, hoping it wouldn't detect her movement.

"What are you doing, Martin? You're going to wake the entire house," a voice whispered.

Another answered apologetically. "It was her watercolor tin. I didn't realize it was hanging off the edge of her desk and I stepped on it."

Eleanor heard an exasperated sigh. "Are you all right?"

"Fine."

"Get to it, then. And be more careful," the first voice said.

Hoping to catch them, Eleanor looked in the direction of her desk before she snapped on the light. She caught a blur, but that was all. "You might as well come out. I know you're here."

Nothing.

"I *heard* you. Come on out."

"Confound it, Martin. Now look what you've done," said the voice. A tiny person emerged from behind her closet door.

Less than a foot high, a woman in an old-fashioned dress bowed to Eleanor. She looked annoyed, and recited in a flat voice:

Brownie, Brownie
Quick, quick, quick
I tend your home
With my broomstick
See me, catch me
I am yours
Until another
Sees me,
Of course

"My name is Brighty. At your service." The woman's tone implied she'd rather stick a fork in Eleanor's eye.

"Where's Martin?" Eleanor asked.

"Come on out, Martin," Brighty said. She wasn't pleased.

Eleanor felt sorry for Martin, but when he stepped from behind the hamper she felt even sorrier. A long nose appeared first, and pulled the rest of him along with it. Thin and balding, his shirt was untucked on one side and his pant leg was torn. He withered under Brighty's glare, and Eleanor could tell he was dreading a tongue-lashing.

"How may we serve you?" Brighty asked in the same snotty, monotone voice.

"I'm wondering why you're in my room."

"Tidying," Brighty said.

"Do you tidy our house every night?"

"*Our* house. Yes."

Eleanor ignored the correction. It wouldn't do to be on this woman's bad side, small though she may be. "Are there more of you?"

Brighty scowled. "You think two of us should be able to care for a house of this size? With four children?"

"Well, no, that isn't what I m—"

Brighty sniffed, and walked out the door. She didn't turn around, but snapped, "Come *on*, Martin."

Martin gave Eleanor a shy look before he scurried out the door.

So there *were* Brownies. Patters was correct. She clicked off the light.

Sleep eluded her, though. The images from Gunnr's mind and her nightmare replayed themselves in her head. After a few minutes, she gave up and clicked the light back on. She grabbed her sketchpad and a pencil, plumped her pillows and stared at the blank page. Motte was the most interesting thing she'd seen, but sketching the sullen Gargoyle didn't appeal to Eleanor. She turned her attention to the Pyskes, and her hand moved across the page of its own accord. She drew Felix, Trinket, and a swarm of Pyske children surrounding them. Little wings, little faces, and little bodies darted across the page. After a while Eleanor felt sleepy, slid lower in her bed and sketched leaning on one arm for a few minutes more. It became harder and harder to stay awake. Finally, the pencil fell from her fingers as sleep overtook her.

"Pull that sail in, Rob. It's luffing." Jack straddled the tiller, craning to see past the sailboat obstructing his view of the channel.

Rob rolled his eyes at Eleanor and Flora. Tightening the sail wouldn't capture nonexistent wind. They needed to get beyond the harbor and into the bay. The sails were so slack Rob didn't even need to uncleat the line to tighten them. He pulled the sheet barehanded and threw another loop around the winch. "This is a waste of time, Jack. Better wind in the afternoon."

"We'll be fine as soon as we get out of the harbor. And besides, we need to be back in time to go with Eleanor and Gunnr."

"Who invited you?" Eleanor asked.

Jack grinned.

Eleanor shrugged. "If we're gonna go sailing, we have to go this morning. I only have the first part of the day, and I want to snoop around Lime Island," she said, referring to the small island on which Camedon said Doris lived.

Abandoned by all but nesting ospreys, the island was a well-kept secret among local residents. A long beach, old granite foundations, and trails through the island's interior attracted explorers, old and young alike.

Seaton's head broke the surface. "Hullo, mates. Where we off to this morning?"

"Just out to Lime," Rob answered

"What'chu wanna go there fer? Doris's cave is there."

"That's why—"

Eleanor cut Rob off. "We're meeting a bunch of friends at that beach. We go every year. It's kinda become a tradition to begin our summer vacation with a picnic on the island."

"Huh. I'd take a cold, rocky beach any day over a sandy beach near Doris. Mean old woman. She's just a mean old woman." With that, Seaton disappeared.

"Why'd you cut me off?"

"I don't know. I didn't think we should be telling him what we're doing," Eleanor said.

They cleared the mouth of the harbor and a breeze rippled across the water. The boat heeled slightly with the gust.

"More sail!" Jack ordered.

"You don't have to yell," Rob muttered, and gave the sail just enough slack to catch the wind. Satisfied, he cleated it.

"Don't cleat that—the wind is only going to increase," Jack said.

Eleanor could tell Rob was done with Jack's orders, but before he could say anything, Flora jumped in. "I'll hold the line."

"You don't have gloves on, Florie," Rob reminded her. "I've got it."

The wind was out of the southeast, and Jack didn't have to cross it many times to reach the island. Eleanor lifted the centerboard as the boat slid onto the beach. They climbed out, and the boys dragged it out of the surf. Flora ran a line from the bow chock to a tree in case the tide rose.

Eleanor lugged their cooler up the beach and set it beneath the trees. "'Kay. Where do you want to start?"

"We could have sailed around the island and decided where to start," Jack said. "We didn't need to walk."

"Suck it up, Jack," Eleanor said. "It's all beach. There's only one spot with rock and ledge. I say we start there."

"Fine." Jack trudged in that direction. Eleanor grabbed a few bottles of water, and they set off after him.

It wasn't far from where they'd beached the boat. Rob gave Flora a boost so she could examine the top of the rock formation. Jack waded in the water, feeling each rock face and the crevices below the surface. He moved aside clumps of floating seaweed and felt under them. Eleanor and Rob walked along a rise in the middle of the rocks.

They searched the ledges for a good twenty minutes, and finally Jack sat on a rock. "The only thing here is a bunch of starfish." He reached down and picked one up.

"Maybe her cave isn't actually on the island," Rob said.

"Maybe it's underwater. Just offshore."

Eleanor studied the rock. It reminded her of the ledge in the cavern, but without the protections. A thought occurred to her. "Wait a minute—maybe we just can't see it. Maybe it's hidden from us!"

Rob and Jack gave her questioning looks, and then Rob got it. "Ask him."

"Ask who?" asked Jack.

Flora climbed down and sat beside Rob. "Camedon?"

"No. Gunnr." Rob was excited. "Ask him!" he urged Eleanor.

"'Kay, hold on." Eleanor closed her eyes and reached for Gunnr. At first she didn't feel him. She focused, picturing him in her mind, and her in his, and spoke to him.

"*Knock, knock,*" she said, tentatively.

"*Mmm?*" he sounded drowsy.

"*Are you awake?*"

"*I am now.*"

"*I need your help.*"

"*Are you all right?*" he asked, his voice no longer sleepy.

"*I'm fine. We're on Lime Island, looking for Doris's cave, and I need you to look at the rocks. See if there are any protections placed on them.*"

"*You're not serious?*"

"*I am.*"

"*Do you have any idea what Doris is capable of? She isn't a grouchy old lady neighborhood kids torment on Halloween, Eleanor. She's a witch, and a powerful one.*"

"*I know. We just want to ask her a few questions.*"

He sighed.

"*Please?*"

"*Fine, I'll look, but even if I'm able to see her magic, it's*" *unlikely I would know how to remove her protections. Or that I would."*

"That's okay. Just look," Eleanor said.

Eleanor climbed off the rock and waded into the water. She stepped back so all of the ledges were in her field of vision. She waited, tense, and reminded herself to relax.

After a moment an image appeared in her mind, superimposed over what she saw before her. Course green woven protections glowed across the rock.

"Yes! This is it!" she said aloud. Rob and Jack scrambled off the rocks and entered the water, examining the face.

"There. You've found the entrance to her cave. I'll tell Camedon. And where are your guards?"

"I have no idea," she told him.

"Hmm." He paused. *"Go home, Eleanor. You have no idea what you're dealing with. Doris isn't stable, nor does she care about observing relations within the Realm."*

"Okay."

Suspicious of her quick acceptance, he asked, *"Okay?"*

"Yeah. We're curious, not stupid. We thought we might find something, but it's obvious her cave is well protected." She added, *"It's hot. We'll go for a swim, and head back. Are we still meeting this afternoon?"*

"Yes."

"The others want to come."

"That's fine."

"Thanks. Sorry to disturb you. We'll see you later?"

Again, she felt his uncertainty. She could almost see suspicion narrowing his eyes. Finally he said, *"Yes,"* and was gone.

She looked at the others.

"So ...?" asked Jack.

"There are protections on these rocks. This probably is the entrance to her cave—or one of them. He said he couldn't remove them, but he'd say that anyway. Oh, he said you guys could come today."

"So we can't get in," Jack concluded. He ripped the starfish in his hands in half and tossed both pieces into the water.

Flora gasped.

"Jack!" Eleanor said. "What did you do *that* for?"

"What? They regenerate. Now there are *two* starfish," he said, unrepentant.

Eleanor shook her head, disgusted.

"So what do we do now?" Rob asked.

Eleanor was at a loss. "Maybe she'll come back, or out, or something."

"And serve us tea? Yeah, okay, Eleanor."

"Enough, Jack," Rob said. "It was worth a try."

Camedon materialized next to Flora with a loud *POP*.

"I'll say one thing for you, guy," Jack said. "Your timing is excellent. That was quick."

The Keeper gave him a dry look. "Gunnr suggested I not dally. He seemed to think you might do something to annoy Doris." The corner of Camedon's mouth twitched. "I can't imagine why." Then he added, "Never a good idea, annoying Doris."

"Let's go in," Jack said.

"*We* aren't going to go in. *I'm* going to go in. You're waiting here." The Keeper floated from the top of the ledge to entrance below.

"We don't want to wait here," Jack said.

Camedon ignored him. He studied the rock face for a moment before raising his hands and removing the protections in a complicated series of movements. He stepped through the rock. Jack and Rob followed, right on his heels.

Eleanor stepped to follow as well, but then remembered Flora, and couldn't leave her alone on the beach.

"Why don't you come here, Florie? Quick, like a bunny," Eleanor encouraged her, keeping an eye on the section of the rock face into which the others had disappeared.

Flora scrambled down and Eleanor took her hand. She didn't want to walk into the ledge face first, so she cautiously extended her hand. It moved through the stone, so Eleanor continued and pulled Flora with her.

They entered a dim, low-ceilinged cavern. Formed from limestone, the walls and ceiling were pale. The tide entered freely through the rock illusion and a shallow river wound throughout the cavern. Shipwreck debris littered the gravel banks and ledges beside the tidal flow. Trunks, cannons, and smaller items lay everywhere: dishes, clothes, jewelry, tattered books, lanterns, hardware, and even a chessboard.

Rob looked around the cavern and let out a low whistle. "Check this place out."

Figureheads leaned against walls, their faces eerie sentinels ringing the cavern.

"Doris? Are you here?" Camedon called. His voice echoed throughout, but went unanswered.

"Where do you think she is?" Eleanor asked.

"Oh, she could be anywhere. We should wait outside. She'll be furious we entered."

"How big is this place? Maybe she didn't hear you."

"I suppose I could peek in a bit farther," Camedon said. "Wait here."

Jack snorted. "In case she shows up? I don't think so."

Taking care not to trip on the scattered items, they followed

Camedon farther into the cavern. Larger on the inside than it appeared from the entrance, the cavern wound beneath the island in a series of chambers and passages. Salvaged debris decorated columns of limestone throughout. Far back, a shaft of sunlight broke the dim interior. They made their way to it and looked up through a rectangular hole.

"This must be an old chimney," Rob said. "That opens to the crumbled foundations? In the center of the island?"

"Yes," Camedon agreed. "You're right."

"I think we should wait outside," Flora suggested in a quiet voice.

Eleanor reached out and took her hand. "We're fine, Florie."

"Flora's right. Doris won't appreciate our intrusion, and won't supply the answers I need if she's angry." Camedon turned in the direction they'd come and stopped short.

Doris was behind them, blocking the passage. "No, she won't," the witch said, face flushed and eyes bulging. "How did you enter? *Why* did you enter?"

Camedon held his hands up. "Don't be angry, Doris. We mean no harm. I have a problem and I need your help."

"Why would I help you?"

"Because the Alabaster Chalice was not in the box you gave me. Newlin is coming and I need answers."

The witches face drained of color. "But it was. It has to be! It's been here since I took it from the Rachel Parker."

"Well, it wasn't, and we need to figure out where it is. Not only because of Newlin, but because it can't be lying around unprotected. Now think," he urged her. "Who knew you had the Chalice?"

"No one."

"Who comes here?"

"No one ever comes here. Only Nob, but he didn't know it was here, and he'd have no reason to take it even if he did know."

The witch turned abruptly and swam back through the cavern, muttering to herself. Camedon and the kids followed. She paused and looked into each chamber she passed before moving to the next. Suddenly she veered and returned to a chamber she'd dismissed.

They didn't follow her in, but hung back, giving her plenty of room. She seemed to forget they were there, talking to herself and gesticulating the entire time. She swam to the rear and pulled her body up the bank to the crates stacked against the wall.

"Do you need assistance?" Camedon asked.

"No." She rifled and rummaged for several minutes, and then, just as quickly, abandoned the chamber and went to another. She looked on shelves, in bins, and behind barrels. A cackle of triumph echoed in the cavern.

She held out a weathered box. "I knew I still had it!" She slithered back down the bank and swam to them, propelled by her thick tail.

"What is it?"

"The set of navigational tools from the Rachel Parker."

"I believe you took what you thought to be the Alabaster Chalice from the Rachel Parker, Doris. I don't require proof."

Doris opened the box. "Oh, it was the Chalice—I held it in my hands. But these aren't just *any* tools, Keeper. This set of navigational tools is magical. See the sight vanes on this sextant?" She pointed to the thin cylindrical tubes on the triangular metal instrument.

Camedon nodded.

"Magical. Newlin had the Dwarves imbue navigational magic into them so the captain of the Rachel Parker would not lose his bearing with his precious cargo."

"Interesting, but I'm more concerned about the location of the Alabaster Chalice."

"Use this." Her thick gray fingers fumbled with a leather pouch, stiffened with age and salt, on the inside of the box. Finally, she worked something free and held it out to him.

"What's that?" Exasperation crept into Camedon's voice.

"Magic. This compass will find the Chalice."

"How?"

"I don't know," she said, and she didn't look like she cared, either. "Something to do with the Lubber's Line. Or the water. Ask Newlin. Now get out, and take the urchins with you."

She harrumphed, herding them toward the entrance to her cavern. Camedon closed the box and secured the fastening, and moved the kids toward the exit.

"I'll return the navigational tools in good stead."

"Don't bother." She swam back into the depths of her cavern.

Chapter Twelve

"Do you want to sail back with us?" Jack asked the Keeper.

Camedon glanced at the water. "Nope, and don't dally. I smell a storm."

Jack looked down the bay with a frown. "It's beautiful out—"

A *POP* interrupted his objection and the Keeper was gone.

They untied the boat and dragged it into the surf. Rob and Jack held it in the waves while Flora and Eleanor raised the sails. As soon as the sails were ready to take wind, Rob and Jack pushed the boat farther into the water and jumped in. It took a minute to get settled, but soon they had a heading for the harbor.

"Look! Storm petrels." Rob pointed.

Hundreds of birds bobbed off their port bow, riding the gentle swells. Someone unfamiliar with New England waters might linger and observe the birds, but the kids knew the flock was only this far up the bay because they sought shelter from incoming weather.

"Sonuvabitch, Camedon was right." Jack said, pointing to wisps of fog reaching up the bay. Behind those wisps, a dark, impenetrable wall obliterated everything beyond. It was ominous, and Eleanor shivered. The sunshine would deteriorate quickly. Instinctively, they each glanced at the sea, sails, and distance to the harbor.

"We'll make it," Jack said. "Rob, pull the jib in, I'm going to head up as high as I can. Flora, move over with Rob. We'll heel when he tightens that sail, so we need ballast. Flat boat's a fast boat." Jack repeated the last under his breath. It was his racing mantra.

He was all business. Eleanor would never admit it, especially to him, but she enjoyed sailing with Jack. The sea brought out the side of him Eleanor liked most, but rarely saw on land. The wind and sea blew away needling Jack and left confident, capable Jack in his stead.

The boat cut through the waves, splashing salty spray in their faces. Sitting farthest forward, Flora got the worst, but the sun was warm and she laughed each time water came over the bow. Eleanor knew Jack was hitting the swells sideways on purpose. Water didn't come over Jack's bow unless he meant for it to. He knew how to ride the rolling swells and cut through water clean as you please. The upturned corner of his mouth confirmed her suspicions. He was playing.

As they entered the harbor, the channel was busy. Other boats were heeding the darkening skies and seeking the safety of their moorings. Jack, tall at the tiller, deftly moved the boat between the larger craft and cut toward their home. They'd left the whaler on the mooring. Jack kept it off his beam and approached two boat lengths below. He cut into the wind at precisely the right moment and slid alongside, drifting to a stop. Rob jumped into the whaler, tossed Jack its bowline and Eleanor the mooring pennant, and climbed back in to help.

"Hop in the whaler, Flora, while we drop the sails," Jack said. "Let's bag 'em instead of furl 'em. I'll hang them in the boathouse to dry."

Rob set Flora in the whaler. Keeping an eye on the sky, he and Eleanor were quick dropping the sails and stuffing them into the sail bag. The fog was now visible at the harbor's mouth. They secured the halyards to the mast, and got out so Jack could give the boat a last check. He tested the lash on the tiller, making sure there was no slack in the mainsail sheet, checked the pennant, and jumped into the whaler with the others.

Eleanor shoved off and Rob headed into the dock.

"We should leave this on the outhaul," Eleanor said. "If we get any weather, it'll bang on the float."

"Mmm," Rob agreed, paying more attention to his approach to the dock. Jack was ready and jumped onto the float as the whaler slid alongside. Eleanor threw their stuff up, helped Flora out, and followed.

Rob attached the outhaul to the stern and Jack took the other line to the whaler's bow. He bent to attach it and lurched back, landing on his rear end.

Nob stared at him.

Rob quickly climbed out of the small whaler and onto the larger float.

"Where is the Keeper?" the Sea Dragon rumbled.

"Don't know," Jack answered.

"Tell him I was here."

"Um, sure. When we see him," Jack stammered.

The Dragon blew, and his head sank below the surface leaving a small swirl.

Jack swallowed. "I *really* don't like that thing," he said.

Baelhar materialized on the float. "I don't think he's particularly fond of you, either," he said. "Gave us the slip this morning, didn't you?"

Jack sat back and looked at the Elf. "I don't know what you mean."

"Wasn't it you who said Flora had walked to the Lee?" Baelhar raised an eyebrow.

Jack grinned. "Oh, yeah. She was in the kitchen, after all."

Baelhar vanished, but delivered a parting, disembodied threat. "Glue, Jack. Just like glue."

Jack gave Rob and Eleanor a sheepish grin. "Worth a shot," he said.

Eleanor shook her head. "Geez, Jack. Grow up. Take our life jackets for us." She dropped hers on Flora's, grabbed the cooler, and headed to the lawn. Rob gave Jack a thumbs up behind her back.

"I saw that," Baelhar's disembodied voice noted.

"Hurry up, you guys. I want to catch Mum and Dad before they leave," Eleanor called over her shoulder. Flora hurried behind her.

"Help me hang these things?" Jack asked his brother.

"Yep." Rob hoisted the sail bag and they climbed the incline to the dock.

The boathouse faced the beach. Long and low, and the doors on the waterside were wide enough to accommodate small boats. The inside was spare. Lidded storage benches lined the sides, and lines crisscrossed the rafters. Jack strung the sails to dry, and hung the life jackets on hooks. Rob checked to make sure the doors facing the water were secure, and they headed to the house. The sun had disappeared, and the air was damp and chilly.

"We made it back just in time," Jack said.

"Eh. We're going with Eleanor anyway."

They entered through the library and heard voices in the hall. Their parents waited, ready to leave, with Charlotte Bradford, Eleanor, and Flora.

"There you are," their mother said. "Good. I was just telling Eleanor and Flora the same rules apply. In by eight o'clock at night. No daytime TV, and *do not* forget your chores in the barn. I told Nickerson he could count on you, and I expect you to do those first thing every morning, and check with him before you take off. Make sure Mrs. Bradford knows where you are. All the time."

"We will, Mum," Eleanor assured her.

"We'll be fine, Ginny," Charlotte said. "You and Peter have a lovely time and call us when you arrive."

"Okay."

Their parents hugged and kissed each of the kids, giving Flora an extra squeeze, and Dr. Driscoll pulled his wife out to the car.

"Hang on!" Jack stopped them. "How come you don't have Camedon take you to Houston through a passage?"

Everyone paused.

"Boy's got a point," her father said.

"Because this is *my vacation.* That's why. Now let's go." Eleanor's mother gave her husband a disapproving look and left. He followed, but Eleanor could tell he was still thinking about Jack's idea.

Rob closed the door behind them.

"Aw-right, let's order pizza," Jack said.

"That's exactly what I was thinking," the librarian said. "Now might be a good time to tell you I don't cook."

The kids grinned.

"Sch-weeeet!" Jack said.

Eleanor glanced at the clock in the foyer. "Guys? Gunnr'll be here soon. You still coming?"

"Yep," Rob said.

"Why don't you three go?" Charlotte said. "I have to go back to the library for a while, and I was hoping Flora might come with me. What do you say, Flora? We'll get the pizza on the way back and you can order anchovies for Jack."

"Sure." Flora grinned.

Jack pulled her braid.

Charlotte held the door for Flora, and said to the older three, "No hurry. Ovens keep pizza warm."

As soon as the door shut, Jack said, "Now *that's* my kinda babysitter."

Eleanor wasn't paying attention, though. She was reaching for Gunnr in her mind.

Chapter Thirteen

"**ARE YOU COMING HERE?**" ELEANOR ASKED GUNNR.

"*Meet me at the cavern.*"

"El?" Jack waved his hand in front of her face. "Earth to Eleanor?"

Eleanor held up her hand. "Hang on."

"*Now?*" Eleanor asked.

"*Yes. I'll be right there. Wear warm clothes. It's wet out.*"

"*What are we doing?*" She sensed his smile.

"*You'll see.*"

"Gunnr said to wear something warm and meet him in the cavern," she told the boys and headed upstairs.

"Now? What are we doing?" Rob asked.

"Beats me. Hurry up."

Eleanor ran to her room and changed to jeans, a turtleneck, and her hikers. She left her clothes where she dropped them and hurried back downstairs. She grabbed her fleece, thought to grab a cap, and pulled her ponytail through the hole in the back.

Rob and Jack thundered down the stairs.

Eleanor tossed them their jackets. "Ready?"

"Yep, let's go."

Baelhar waited on the terrace in a wicker chair, legs stretched and crossed at the ankles. He stood when they stepped out. "Shall we, my young charges? Anyone need to use the potty before we go? Jack?"

Jack smirked. "Heh. Still peeved I sent you on a wild goose chase?"

"Two Elves refused to come back. Now I have double duty."

Jack's grin grew. "Two down, three to go."

"Your parents are gone, Jackie, and there's a new sheriff in town. Pester me at your own risk." Baelhar headed down the granite steps.

The kids followed, and as they passed the flowerbeds, Eleanor heard humming. She paused and looked closer. Pyskes darted amongst the flowers. Some perched on the blossoms like butterflies, some were weeding, and some shook flower blossoms. A cloud of dust surrounded the activity.

"Hello!" one greeted her, zipping up to Eleanor's face. A scrap of yellow cloth, tied bandana fashion, held the Pyske's hair out of her eyes. She had dirt on one cheek.

"Hi," Eleanor said. "Who are you?"

"Fleck."

"Hi, Fleck. I'm Eleanor."

"I know," the Pyske said, tilting her head and smiling as if Eleanor were daft.

"You're busy."

"Tending. Gathering pollen. Before the storm."

"Pollen?"

"For winter," the Pyske prompted, as if Eleanor should have known. She darted away, leaving a trail of dust behind her.

"El?" Rob asked, waiting.

Baelhar and Jack were halfway to the beach. She and Rob hurried to catch them.

The day had deteriorated, even since they'd brought the boat in. Gone was that morning's sunshine, replaced by heavy fog and weather from the south. The wind was up, and the Coast Guard buoy out in the bay groaned with each swell it rode. Eleanor's cheeks were wet. She was glad she'd thought to pull on a hat and change to hikers. The rocks on the beach were slick.

Gunnr waited inside the cavern.

"They're your problem now," Baelhar greeted him cheerfully. Gunnr's mouth quirked. "Not so fast. I need some help. I promised Eleanor we'd practice physical defense."

Baelhar sighed.

Eleanor studied the two, remembering Sehlis saying they'd been inseparable when they were young. They differed in appearance. Where Gunnr had dark, wavy hair, Baelhar's was a brownish-blond, and shoulder-length. Baelhar was as angular as Gunnr, as all Elves tended to be, but he was an inch or so shorter, with a wider stature. His shoulders and upper body were broad, as was his face with its cleft chin. Gunnr was taller and leaner.

Baelhar's expression was sardonic, amused, while Gunnr's was more serious and weighted. Eleanor couldn't help but compare the two men, and she wondered what they'd been like when they were young. Had Gunnr been more like Baelhar then? Before he'd participated in the ritual? She thought of Rob and Jack, who were different, but so close. Had Gunnr and Baelhar gotten in trouble? Who'd been the instigator, or had they been equally culpable?

Gunnr's exile troubled her. She felt as if she'd lost something, but she didn't know what. So many years and so much sadness. His, with all of his years alone, and his family and friends, losing him as surely as if he'd died. She mourned for the boys these men had been.

"Eleanor. Stop!"

Gunnr's words brought her out of herself. Everyone was staring at her. Gunnr with concern, Baelhar contemplative, and

Jack and Rob puzzled.

"I see what you mean," Baelhar said to Gunnr. "We left her exposed yesterday, didn't we?"

A muscle twitched in Gunnr's jaw. Eleanor had a hard time reading his expression, but she knew she'd crossed a line.

"Sorry."

"You needn't apologize. I'm not used to this either, Eleanor."

If anything, his words made her feel worse. He closed his mind to her, and she felt hollow. Alone. She'd grown used to him staying in a corner of her mind. Used to not having to reach for him.

"Where is Flora?" Gunnr asked the boys.

"She went with Mrs. Bradford."

"Just as well. I promised Eleanor I'd teach her how to defend herself, but Flora is rather young for what I had in mind. Shall we?" He took Eleanor's hand and walked through the rock face.

A high-ceilinged area waited on the other side of the passage. Timbers framed the heights, but the floor was packed dirt. Thick ropes cordoned two rings in the middle of the hall.

Baelhar, holding Rob's and Jack's hands, stepped out a moment later.

"Where are we?" Eleanor asked.

"Tunnel three," he said.

Eleanor frowned and looked around for Motte.

Weapons of all kinds and ages adorned the walls. Spears, battleaxes, shields, swords, and crossbows, maces, and war hammers. Protective mail, gauntlets, and masks hung beside the appropriate weapons. Eleanor couldn't decide if it was a museum or a gym.

Jack looked around and whistled. "Dude. This is so cool." He and Rob wandered farther into the hall examining the arms, fascinated.

Gunnr went to a rough-hewn table, chose a few knives, and handed one to each.

Eleanor palmed hers. The blade was oversized and a piece extended where a handle ordinarily would be, but there was no handle, only holes in the flat metal. "What are these?"

"Really?" Baelhar looked at Gunnr. "Today?" He gripped the bridge of his nose.

Gunnr smiled at his friend. "Yes." He explained to the kids, "You are going to learn to throw knives. Humans don't have the strength others of the Realm have, and, you're young Humans, at that. You'd never be able to overpower an attacker. Your best defense is to strike from a distance. Baelhar here is going to teach you how."

"Let me see one of those." Baelhar took Rob's knife and played with it, feeling its weight. He held it lightly by the tip of the blade and ran his finger along the edge. Without warning he spun and threw the knife. It hit the wall with a hollow thoo-pp, impaled in the wood.

"Nice balance. You make these?"

"Yep."

"Iron is hard to learn with. Why not steel?"

"If they can throw iron, they can throw anything. We'll start them with the knives. They might prefer stars." Gunnr shrugged. "But they need to learn to throw first."

"Stars!" Jack said, excited, and Baelhar chuckled.

Baelhar walked over to the far end of the hall. On the wall were thick mats with a row of targets. He loosened his shoulders, and rolled his neck. "Loose. You have to be loose, relaxed. Keep your eye on the target. Every weapon is different and you have to feel it. Its weight, its size. Once you decide what you like, you'll need to practice. You can't pick up any old knife and throw it."

"You just did."

Baelhar tilted his head, and smiled. He held the knife blade between his thumb and index knuckle. "You'd hold this one like this. Loose. Keep your arm loose. You ever throw darts?"

"Yep," Rob and Jack both said, and Eleanor nodded.

"It's like that. Pull your arm back, and keeping your eye on the target, let her fly."

Thoo-p. The knife landed dead center.

"Come here, Rob." Baelhar pulled Rob in front of him, and positioned his arms. "That's right, loose. Eye the target …"

Rob threw the knife. It bounced off the wall and landed on the floor. Neither Jack nor Eleanor laughed. They were glad Rob had gone first.

"Not bad. It actually hit the outside of the target. Step into it, and give it some wrist action on the release. Jack, Eleanor, pick another target." Baelhar pointed to two far enough away from each other, and gave them each several knives.

Gunnr leaned against the wall, watching, a half smile on his face. He was enjoying this, and Eleanor suspected he and Baelhar had done this many times before.

Baelhar stood behind Jack and tapped his shoulder reminding him to drop them. Jack threw. It sunk into the mat, but next to Rob's target five feet away. Jack bit the inside of his lip, narrowed his eyes, and let another fly. This one hit his own target, but handle first, and bounced off.

"Keep trying. Your posture's good, Jack. Check each other before you retrieve your knives," Baelhar reminded them as he moved behind Eleanor.

"Loose. Stay loose. That's it," Baelhar said.

"Send it true, just like your light. Aim it. Focus it."

Eleanor didn't acknowledge him. She thought about Eilvain, the vampire who'd attacked her. Pictured the target as the Noctivagus's torso. She eyed it, imagining a laser beam between her hand and the target, and threw. The knife sunk into the mat inside the largest circle of the target.

She looked over at Rob and Jack and smirked.

"Lucky throw," Rob said.

She threw another. It stuck, closer to the target's center than the last.

"Attagirl."

"Watch and learn, boys," Baelhar said. "Your sister's getting it."

"Yeah, she always wins at darts, too," Jack said. He threw another, and this one stuck into his target.

"Pool, too," Rob said, and released his. It didn't even hit the mat.

"Concentrate. You're throwing wild. Keep your eye on the target until the knife hits. Step into it, and follow completely through, with your energy and your eye."

Eleanor threw her last three knives. One hit and stuck. The other two hit but bounced off. She waited for her brothers to throw theirs before retrieving hers.

"Keep practicing," Gunnr said. "I want to show Baelhar something—we'll be right back."

Eleanor, Rob, and Jack continued to throw with increasing accuracy. Eleanor threw consistently better than her brothers, and that was satisfying, but they were hitting the target more times than not.

Gunnr and Baelhar returned. They observed for a few minutes before Gunnr returned to the long table and grabbed different knives.

"Try these," he said, handing them out. These knives were smaller, but the blades were larger, heavier. The knife was mostly blade.

Eleanor weighed it in her hand. Completely different in shape and weight. She aimed and threw. Its weight made it fly faster, and hit the target handle first.

"Drop your shoulders. Find your center." Gunnr pushed her shoulders down and pulled her arm tighter to her body.

She threw, and again it bounced off.

"More snap on the release. Again."

"Hey, can't you just give us magic knives?" asked Jack.

"Sure. But this is more fun." Gunnr took Eleanor's knives and threw them in rapid order. He hit each of the kids' targets dead center, thunk, thunk, thunk, down the line.

Baelhar let out a short laugh and took Jack's knives. He threw three as fast. They hit perfectly above Gunnr's, but sideways, and the two together formed crossed T's.

Rob walked over to Gunnr and handed his over. Gunnr smiled, accepting the challenge. He threw them, and they landed above Baelhar's, making each grouping a cross.

"Wanna try stars?" Gunnr asked them.

Rob's and Jack's faces lit up.

He retrieved a smaller sheath from the table, and removed a set of flat, intricate discs. They were slightly smaller than the palm of Eleanor's hand. He fit it into his own palm, sideways. "First rule. Don't do this." He repositioned it on his fingertips and then set his thumb on it. "Like this, or you'll lay your hand wide open. Keep the blades of each point away from you. Get in the habit of finding the edge every single time you look at a star. Train your eye to the edge, and your hand will pick it up correctly."

He moved to Eleanor's target and threw the star overhand. "You can throw it this way, but it's hard on your elbow and shoulder. Your arm has to work harder as it doesn't have your body propelling it. I prefer to throw them like this." He turned sideways, and threw it across his abdomen, like a Frisbee. "The body follows through. Overhand stilts the motion—the energy."

Gunnr handed a star to Eleanor and stepped back. She started to position herself, and he said, "Looser in your knees, and drop your shoulders. That's it. Fluid."

She threw, and it went wide, hitting Jack's target.

"Late release. Take turns at this target. One at a time. We don't need any accidents."

Rob threw and hit the target.

"Good!" Baelhar said.

Jack stepped forward and assumed the position to throw. "Damn!" he said, and held his hand up, revealing a gash welling with blood. Gunnr reached for Jack's hand, but Baelhar cut between them, blocking Gunnr with his body. He took Jack's hand, raised his finger to the wound, and drew a ball of white light over it. The gash *heiled* under the light's passage.

"Thanks," Jack said, scrunching his hand a few times.

There was an awkward silence. Gunnr's smile stayed in place, but his expression tightened. Eleanor felt his withdrawal. Felt his resignation that Baelhar's first thought was to protect Jack from him.

"I think we've practiced enough for tonight. We'll do it again. You can take the knives to practice in your barn. We'll leave the stars here for now." He gathered the stars, took them back to the table, and headed toward the door.

"Jack knows you wouldn't hurt him," Eleanor said.

"Baelhar is your guard. He was doing what he should."

"We don't need protection from you."

He didn't answer her, but kept walking toward the door.

"Gunnr?"

"It's fine. Really," he assured her. His tone was even, but he pulled away from her and closed his mind.

"Would you take them back?" he asked Baelhar. At Baelhar's nod, he left.

Eleanor turned on Baelhar. "What was that?"

"What?"

"You jumping between Gunnr and Jack. Jack doesn't need protection from him," Eleanor's scathing tone got Baelhar's attention and his eyebrow arched.

"Apparently not. But I didn't know that, now, did I?" he said, unconcerned.

Eleanor crossed her arms. "You know what? I'm done with this. I ignored Sehlis's coolness the other day, but I saw it. And I saw the same attitude at the Gathering."

"Gladstone—"

"Gladstone nothing. No one stuck up for him. Everyone sat there and let it go on. Enough. The Realm is quick to turn to him when they need help, but he isn't good enough to acknowledge after he fixes your problem. I'm done. No more dumb lessons, no more guards, no more *nothing*. I'm done. You tell Queen Solvanha that."

Rob and Jack stared, speechless, but Eleanor didn't care.

Baelhar assessed her for several moments. She didn't look away, but met him stare for stare.

His eyes narrowed. "From the mouths of babes."

"What's *that* supposed to mean?"

"You're right, of course."

His words caught her off guard.

"He is a Warrior of the Realm and should be treated as such. I will speak with Queen Solvanha and the council."

"Do whatever you want. I'm done here. I want to go home."

Rob and Jack must have been stunned by her outburst, but she didn't care. She strode to the door, but no one had followed. "You coming or what?"

She followed the hall to the Nave and sat on the platform fuming.

"That was quite a show," a bored voice intoned.

Eleanor looked around. Motte's outline grew more substantial on one of the pediments.

"He doesn't need you to defend him."

"And I don't need any crap from you, either," Eleanor said.

Motte laughed, but it was more of a dry wheeze.

"Open the passage, would you? I'd like to go home."

"No."

"Why not?"

"Much as your presence grates, it would displease him if I allowed you to leave unattended," Motte said.

Eleanor caught the undertone of unattended. Motte might as well have said off-leash. Eleanor knew there wasn't any sense in arguing, and Rob, Jack, and Baelhar approached anyway. She stood.

"Let's go." She headed for the passage in tunnel two, and waited for them at the rock face. Baelhar reached for her hand, but she took Rob's instead. He didn't seem annoyed at her dismissal, but amused.

"Just go," she instructed him.

He stepped through the passage, and they followed. Once through, she dropped Rob's hand and marched out of the cavern, not caring if anyone followed.

Chapter Fourteen

*"**Meet me on the terrace.**"*

"*Go away.*" Eleanor rolled over and punched her pillow.

"*Come down. I want to talk to you.*"

"*Nope. I told Baelhar. I'm through. Done.*"

"*You have five minutes to come down, or I'm coming up.*"

"*I don't care. Come on up if you want,*" she said, with a little smile to herself. She knew Mrs. Bradford had locked the doors.

A tap at the window startled her.

Damn.

He was outside her window, leaning on the sill. "*You going to open the window? Shall I knock louder?*" he raised his hand to do so.

Eleanor quickly went to the window. She opened it and stuck her head out. "Go away. I was sleeping."

"No you weren't."

"Go away … anyway."

"No. I want to show you something. Put some warm clothes on."

"I can't just leave. Mrs. Bradford …"

"Knows," Gunnr cut her off. "Don't make me use my *voice*."

"Use your dumb voice. I'm not going," she said, and went back to the bed.

Gunnr bent and stepped into her room. Dressed formally in clothing of the Realm, he wore a white ruffled shirt, breeches, and high boots. A cloak fell to the ground behind him. He went to her bureau and opened drawers until he found jeans and a shirt. He tossed them to her. "You're acting like a sullen teenager."

"I *am* a sullen teenager."

He tipped his head to her point, and smiled, but it didn't reach his eyes. "Get dressed."

She didn't move.

"Please," he added, in a gentler tone. "I have something I want to show you. And grab a jacket. Unless you'd rather I took Jack. Or Rob."

He sat down and waited. She grabbed her clothes and stalked to her bathroom to change.

She returned dressed, put her hikers on, and pulled her hair back into a ponytail. "Fine. I'm ready."

"You need a coat."

"You're sitting on it."

He stood and picked up her jacket. She reached for it, but rather than hand it to her, he held it for her to put on.

"You told Mrs. Bradford?"

"Yes. Charlotte amazes me. Pleasant, even when woken." Gunnr went to the window and held the curtain back. "After you."

Eleanor climbed onto the terrace roof. "I don't think my parents will appreciate you teaching me how to sneak out of the house."

"Your parents aren't stupid enough to think you need me to teach you how to sneak out of the house."

Oh. Formality was over.

"You'll be treated how you act."

"Stop reading my mind!"

"I can't. We need to come to a comfortable place with this. You're only getting stronger, and seeing as how I drew the short straw—"

"That's not very nice."

He smiled. "Again, you'll be treated how you act."

"Me? I'm not the one who jumped between you and Jack today!"

"Baelhar did nothing wrong. It's his job to protect you."

Eleanor made a face and moved to climb back in the window.

He stopped her. "I understand. You were responding to my memories, but you weren't responding to," he searched for the right words, "*mutual* memories. Those are mine, but you assigned them to him, and that wasn't fair, because his are different. Baelhar and I were best friends when we were young, but that was long, long ago, and I betrayed our friendship. Baelhar and I must get to know each other again." He'd closed his mind to her so she couldn't read his thoughts, but the twitching muscle in his jaw belied his casual explanation.

Eleanor considered his words. She disagreed, but opted to be agreeable. "I'm sorry. You're right. I'll try harder to think before I act."

He studied her, seeing things no one else did. Seeing things no one else should. Her thoughts, and her feelings. She looked away, but he tipped her chin up so she couldn't avoid his gaze. "You have nothing to apologize for. We, *you and I*, need to become more comfortable with this connection. It's awkward."

"It's very awkward. I don't know how to think of you."

"What do you mean?"

"Well, you're old."

He smiled.

"But you *look* younger than my parents."

His smile grew. "You might want to keep that observation to yourself."

"You could be like a teacher, or something, but I'm more comfortable with you than I've ever been with any of my teachers. It's sort of like you are family. But you aren't."

He considered her words for a moment before speaking. "Sometimes it helps to define things. Especially strange, new things. For instance, you know exactly what your relationship with your brothers and Flora is. And your parents, and friends. The connection we share doesn't fit neatly in a regular category."

Eleanor nodded. "That's what I mean. Until two weeks ago, you were a stranger, but …" her voice trailed off.

"But it feels as if you've known me for much longer," he finished for her.

"Yes," Eleanor said, frowning. None of this made any sense.

"It's strange for me, too, Eleanor. I didn't see this coming. I didn't see *you* coming." His laugh was dry. "Things have been rather peaceful for the last few centuries."

"You know what I mean."

"I do. Maybe it would help to think of me as, say, an older cousin. Someone you can count on. Someone with, perhaps, better judgment than Jack." He smiled. "We'll keep the bar low."

"You could set it on the ground."

He rubbed his forehead, as if he had a headache, but his tone was gentle when he said, "We're stuck with each other. I don't know why, but there it is, so we'd best learn to deal with it. You'll have to be patient with me, though. With the exception of Motte, my social skills have been neglected for a *very* long time. All right?"

"All right."

He picked her up and, holding her in front of him, flew off.

This flight was very different from the first one he'd taken her on. No moonlight penetrated the thick fog, and she couldn't see anything. It was disconcerting to be moving so fast through a visual void. The air was thick and wet, and she was glad she had her coat as the rushing wind chilled her.

"How can you see in this?"

"I know where I'm going."

"Where *are* we going?"

"To a party."

That got her attention.

He explained. "Newlin, the Undine Prince, has arrived. The Water Sprites are welcoming him with a celebration."

"Nice night for it."

He chuckled. "You think getting wet bothers water spirits?"

"Where is it going to be?"

"By the river."

"Could you be a little more specific? Which part of the river?"

"In the park. No Humans."

That made sense. "Why are we going?"

"Everyone's invited. Even Night Elves. Light Elves and Dwarves are the only Beings who shun Night Elves. I enjoy hospitality among the others," he said, and added, "when I accept it."

"Will I know anyone?" She shivered. She was now soaked and cold.

"We're almost there," he assured her. "Yes. Camedon, and some of the Elves, like Sol, and King Vitr. You said you met Meg?"

"At the river."

They dropped to the ground and landed on the old logging road. He set her on her feet. A glow illuminated the fog in the distance, and she heard noise, but the fog muffled anything identifiable. The moisture falling from the trees was louder.

Gunnr rubbed his hands together, creating a glow of light

and warmth. Passing his hands in front of her, her hair dried, and she felt warmer. She rubbed her arms, and was startled to not feel her fleece, but silky fabric. She looked down. Her jeans were gone, replaced by a filmy skirt. Before she could comment, he swirled a thick cloak behind her and fastened it at her shoulder with a chain.

He stood back, assessing his work. An image of herself entered her mind. She looked very different. Younger with her hair down, she was surprised how much like Flora she looked. She couldn't help but admire the boots. They were just like the ones Sehlis wore. The dress had a scoop neck, and fell delicately in flat pleats to her knees, its smooth line barely interrupted by the wide belt at her hips. She ran her hands over the belt and found a flat leather pouch on the back of her hip.

"Knives?"

"Came with the belt."

"Thank you."

He understood she didn't mean the knives. "We *are* attending a party."

She worked the dress's fabric between her fingers, the softness soothing. "So finely woven, but warm."

"It will stay dry, too."

He kicked the leaves aside, bent, and chose two stones. He clutched them in his hands for several moments, and then handed them to her. They were warm.

"Put these in the pockets inside your cloak."

"Jack's right. Magic rocks. How come you aren't wet?"

"It's an Elven thing."

"What's the protocol with Realm royalty?"

"With Newlin? No protocol. We don't observe the pomp and circumstance Humans do. It's more of a position of service.

Of course we respect those who serve, but there aren't any rings to kiss, or curtsies to make. Ready?"

Their footfalls were silent on the damp leaves as they neared the large gathering. Torches lit and shaped the parameters, and a bonfire burned beside the river. Strung throughout the tree branches, lengths of opalescent fabric shaped the space of merrymaking and glowed in the firelight. She couldn't see the source, but strains of music floated on the fog. The center of the gathering drew her attention: a long table beside the river, behind which a line of fountains erupted from the river's surface. The fountains were lit from within, and water droplets caught the light as they cascaded. It was magical, and a gasp escaped her lips.

"Perfect. The festivities have already begun. We missed his address. We won't stay long—I just want you to see, and be seen."

Eleanor didn't understand and gave him a puzzled look.

"There's much curiosity about your family, and you are apt to be bombarded by attention and scrutiny. Being seen with me will keep some of it at bay. *That's* a Night Elf thing." His short laugh had a bitter edge.

Before Eleanor could respond, Meg spied them and called, "Eleanor!" She left the group she'd been with and made her way through the crowd to them.

"Meg is fine. You may socialize with Meg."

Eleanor's eyebrow shot up. "May?"

"I meant she's fine. You can trust her. Don't mind me. Parties aren't really my thing."

"But you hide it so well," Eleanor muttered. "Hi Meg."

"Welcome. Perfect timing." She leaned in and whispered, "Newlin's finished speaking. H'lo, Gunnr."

He greeted the Sprite, but she'd already returned her attention to Eleanor.

"Have you met him? Newlin?" Meg asked, excited.

Eleanor shook her head. "No."

Gunnr looked toward the table at the river's edge. Eleanor followed his gaze to where Camedon, Queen Solvanha, and King Vitr gathered, along with others she did not recognize, but assumed they were other Elders.

"I'll take her over in a few minutes," Gunnr told Meg.

"Let's go now," the Sprite urged. "I want Eleanor to meet my parents." Meg grabbed Eleanor's hand and dragged her to the table. Gunnr had little choice but to follow.

Eleanor knew she was being examined by those they passed, but she was so busy examining them she didn't mind the scrutiny. Some of the different Beings she recognized from the Solstice ceremony, but many she hadn't seen before. Small, large, winged, and strange, all flaunted their finery. The clothing was richly detailed, and jewelry gleamed in the firelight. Both the men and women wore gold, silver, and jewels. Eleanor was even more grateful Gunnr had fixed her clothing.

"You're welcome."

"How do you know what I'm actually thinking? I can't do that with you."

"I have filters. You don't yet. You could know, though, if you so chose. I'm not blocking you, but rather, toning it down. You could easily see past my filters if you tried."

"I wouldn't do that," she said.

"Sooner or later you will—you won't be able to help it."

"Do all Elves do this?"

His expression became guarded. *"No."*

"So I'm some kind of freak?"

"No."

Camedon stood when he saw them. He clasped Gunnr's forearms in the formal greeting of warriors. King Vitr did as well. Several others Eleanor didn't know stepped forward to greet Gunnr, but in King Vitr's shadow they disappeared. She'd forgotten how large he was. Again, the irony of the Dwarf *dwarfing* everyone struck her.

King Vitr took Eleanor's hand and bowed low over it. "Miss Eleanor. Always a pleasure." The whiskers of his great beard tickled her hand.

Hands grasped her shoulders from behind, and Queen Solvanha gave her an affectionate squeeze. "My dear." The Elven Queen turned her and held her at arm's length. The fair queen resembled her brother's dark looks in only one way. They shared their father's dark blue eyes, which met over Eleanor's head. "Lovely." She gave Gunnr an approving nod. "Come. Meet the Undine Prince."

She led Eleanor to the guest of honor at the table. "Newlin, this is the child I told you about. Eleanor Driscoll."

The prince stood, and Eleanor recognized him from the Solstice Ceremony. He'd stood on one of the points of the Elf Cross.

He reached across to shake Eleanor's hand. "Miss Driscoll." He purposely greeted her in the way of Humans, and Eleanor appreciated the kindness.

"Sir," was all she could think to say.

"Call me Newlin," he said, his casual manner meant to put her at ease.

Eleanor wasn't sure what she'd expected of the man who'd been in love with Doris, but this wasn't it. He appeared perfectly normal. But for his unique eyes, Eleanor might have even mistaken him for Human. The irises were a dark gold, almost the same rich color as his longish, blond hair. His clothes were similar to Elven clothing, and shimmery, but he wore no jewelry or other adornment identifying him as a prince.

"Eleanor, meet my parents," Meg interrupted. "Beg pardon, sir." Meg didn't wait for Newlin to grant his pardon, though, and pulled Eleanor away. "These are my parents. Don't worry about their names—you can't pronounce them anyway. You can call them Mr. and Mrs. Cook. Get it? Megunticook?"

"How do you do?" Eleanor asked. Both had the same color hair as Meg; so pale it was almost white.

Each greeted her kindly, but Meg dragged her away before a conversation could start. "Come on. I have a ton of people I want you to meet."

Eleanor looked to Gunnr.

He nodded. "Stay with Meg."

She followed Meg through the crowd, but it wasn't easy to keep up as the Sprite moved as easily on land as she did in water.

"Can I ask you a question?"

"Yes."

"How old are you?"

"Twenty," Meg said. "We age slower than Humans, though. I am more like your fourteen. Why?"

"I wasn't certain. Most of the Beings I've met are hundreds of years old."

"My parents are, too. Sprites also have longer life spans than Humans." The Sprite giggled. "I was a surprise. My older brother is one-hundred-forty-three years old."

Eleanor pictured Rob at one-hundred-forty-three and laughed.

She was glad to be away from the head table of Elders, but the crowd was thick and Eleanor felt uneasy even with Meg by her side. Conversations died as she passed and Beings stared at her, most with friendly expressions, but some with suspicion. She thought she caught the word Noctivagus. She reached for Gunnr, and felt him holding their connection intact. His reassurance bolstered her.

Meg finally reached a small group on the fringe of the crowd. Eleanor guessed they were Water Sprites like Meg, as they were similar in appearance and dress, but she wasn't certain.

"This is my friend Eleanor. Eleanor, this is Sheila, Vidia, and Mim. They're Sprites, like me. And this is Libbet, Hocke, and Foster. They're Fae."

"Hi," Eleanor said, and received acknowledging smiles.

Hocke stepped toward them, and shielding his hand from view of the crowd, passed Meg a cup. "Filched some mead."

Meg accepted the cup and drank. She handed it to Eleanor to finish. Eleanor took the cup, but hesitated.

"Try it," Meg urged. "Fae mead is fabulous." Eleanor took a small sip. It was delicately sweet, and the swallow warmed all the way to her stomach. She took a larger drink, and handed the cup back to Hocke. He grinned and slipped into the trees where Eleanor suspected he'd hidden more. He confirmed her suspicion a moment later by reappearing and handing a full cup around.

"Eleanor, did I see you arrive with the Night Elf, Gunnr?" Mim asked. Eleanor guessed her to be Meg's age, but she was the smallest one in the group, not even reaching to Eleanor's nose. Her short hair was spikey and appeared wet. It was edgy, and it worked with her pointed face.

Eleanor nodded.

"He's dreamy," Libbet said.

"He's old," Foster snorted. "Probably farts dust."

Eleanor grinned. He reminded her of Jack.

"You *wish* you had an Elven lifespan," Mim said. She took the cup and drained it, and held it to Hocke, wanting more.

Eleanor felt a tug on her cloak and found Simo standing beside her. Happy to see a familiar face, she bent and hugged the small man. "Hi!"

"Wanted to say hello," he said, blushing. He moved on.

"How do you know him?" Meg asked, impressed.

Eleanor really didn't want to say. "We met last month before the Solstice Ceremony."

"Good men, Do-gakw-ho-wad are. Lucky to have one look upon you with favor. Keep to themselves, but good men," Hocke said, offering Eleanor the cup of mead again.

She took another drink and handed it to the Being next to her, Vidia. The Sprite looked at the cup and then at Eleanor, as if she smelled something distasteful, then turned back to Foster. Mim frowned and took the cup. She and Libbet both gave Vidia a reproachful look, but the Sprite either didn't notice, or didn't care.

Eleanor felt awkward. She pulled her cloak around her for comfort, and for something to do. She remembered the stones in her pockets and slid her hands in to warm them.

With her hands in her pockets, she was unable to break her fall when something slammed into her and sent her sprawling.

Chapter Fifteen

SHE HEARD SCREAMING AND PANDEMONIUM. PEOPLE ASKING if she was all right. One voice repeatedly called her name, shook her shoulders, and demanded her attention. She wished whoever it was would stop.

That it was Gunnr finally registered. "Eleanor! *Look at me!*" he demanded, both aloud and in her mind. Her eyes met his, saw the worry and concern, but she couldn't answer, couldn't respond. Nothing was there. No air. She couldn't inhale ... exhale ... her chest was paralyzed. Panic built, paralyzing her even more.

Heiling light flooded her, soothed and warmed her, and she recognized the compulsion layered in his voice when he ordered her to breath. It freed the paralysis in her chest and she inhaled. The deep, desperate breath caused her diaphragm to spasm, and she coughed until she lurched to the side and vomited.

Meg knelt beside Gunnr, patted Eleanor's shoulder, and offered a cloth when she finished. Eleanor took it and wiped her face. She was startled to see blood on the cloth.

"It's not yours. You're fine. Got the wind knocked out of you, but you're fine," Gunnr assured her.

"What happened?" Eleanor asked. She looked around, but all she saw were concerned faces. Fortunately, they were faces she knew. Camedon, Queen Solvanha, and the Sprites and Fae she'd met with Meg. Though unintentional, their concern shielded her from view, and she was grateful. She sunk back to the ground on her elbow, and Meg tugged her cloak up to cushion her head.

"We had gatecrashers. A Noctivagi attack. They flew over and dumped two bodies into the crowd. One hit you. Hard. You dropped like a stone," Foster blurted, impressed.

But the thought of being hit by a body was anything but impressive, and Eleanor rolled to her side and retched again. When she was able to stop she looked around for the body. She saw blood on the ground, but nothing else.

"It's gone," Meg told her. "They removed it."

"Who was it?"

"No one you know."

"Where are they now?"

"The Noctivagi?" Gunnr asked.

She nodded.

"Being pursued by the Warriors who were here. There were several."

"I want to go home," she told Gunnr, and looked to Camedon and Queen Solvanha.

"Another minute, Eleanor. Catch your breath," the Elven Queen urged her. She knelt beside Eleanor. "Such a lovely dress. Let's get you cleaned up." She waved her hands over Eleanor. The stains vanished from her dress, and her face felt free from dirt and grime.

Hocke bent and offered her the cup they'd been sharing a moment before. "Mead? Get the nasty taste out of your mouth. Give 'er a good swish and spit," he encouraged.

"Quite right. Fae mead is good for what ails you," Camedon said.

Eleanor accepted the cup gratefully. She swished her mouth and spat, earning an approving grin from Hocke, but then she took a proper swallow. A large one, and it warmed her insides. They were right. It helped. "Thank you."

"Better?" Gunnr asked.

"Yes."

"Let's get you home, then, shall we?"

"You want me to take her?" Camedon asked.

"No. I'll take her."

"You want me to go with you?"

"Why don't we both go?" Queen Solvanha said.

"It's fine, Sol. The point is close, and the Noctivagi are on the run now. We'll be perfectly safe." He looked around at those who lingered. "I imagine you both have business here, anyway."

At their uncertain expressions, he said, "Really. We'll be fine." Gunnr picked Eleanor up, and Meg tucked her cloak around her. Eleanor gave her an appreciative smile as Gunnr launched himself into the air.

He didn't get far before she said, "I'm going to be sick again."

"Hang on." He dropped, landing close to where they'd arrived earlier, and set her on her feet. She bent over, breathing deeply through her nose and swallowing the saliva pooling. Finally she straightened. "Sorry."

"It's fine," he said. "Bad mead?"

She brightened. "No. I quite liked the mead. I'm ready now. Much better."

She wrapped the cloak around her and Gunnr scooped her up again. This time she was fine and warm, and she relaxed. She turned her face into his shoulder and inhaled. The clean, slightly spicy scent was uniquely his, but it was now as familiar and comforting as her father's wintergreen Lifesavers, or the whiff of perfume that lingered on her mother's pillow.

She felt safe. She may have even dozed, because it seemed

the next moment he landed on the terrace roof. He lifted the window sash with the toe of his boot and set her inside.

"You all set?" he asked.

"Yep."

"Here are your other clothes. Lock the window."

"I will."

"All right? Really?"

"Yes."

He watched her lock it.

"Pull the shade, too."

She pulled the shade and set the bundle of clothes on the desk. Her pajamas were folded neatly on her bed, which had been remade.

She hung her dress, but removed the sheath from the belt and took it to bed with her, sliding it under her pillow. Flora had Bumper. Eleanor had knives.

Sleep came, but it was a restless state. Eleanor tossed, turned, and dreamed dreams she didn't remember. She was unsettled the next morning.

"You look like hell," Jack told her at the breakfast table.

"You're only allowed to swear on the boat, Jackie," Flora reminded him.

"So what are we doing today?" Eleanor asked the table at large.

"You'll have to fend for yourselves, I'm afraid. I'm at the library," Charlotte said.

"Skies've cleared. I'm going out. Who's going with me?" asked Jack.

"I will!" Flora said.

Rob looked at Eleanor. "You wanna go?"

"I guess. I don't know. I might go back to bed," Eleanor

said, yawning.

"What's the matter with you?"

"Gunnr came back last night and took me to the welcome celebration for the Undine Prince."

"What the—"

Flora cleared her throat.

"Heck," Jack said. "How come you got to go and we didn't?" Jack was steamed.

Eleanor looked at Rob. He was annoyed, too. She put her hands up. "Don't yell at me. It wasn't my idea."

Charlotte interrupted. "It was last minute. I didn't go, either."

Jack hardly looked mollified. He glared at Eleanor.

"What's that look for?"

"How come *you* always get to go?"

Eleanor had had it. "You know what, Jack? You wanna go next time? Fine with me. I didn't ask for this. I don't want people in my head. You think this is so cool? Spoiler alert—it isn't a video game. It's real and it's nasty." Eleanor got up from the table and pushed her chair in. "I'm going back to bed." She left the dining room.

"Eleanor?" Flora called after her.

Mrs. Bradford said, "She's fine, dear. Let her go."

Eleanor shut her door and climbed into bed. The room was too bright, so she got up again and shut the shades she'd opened earlier. Better. The dark room matched her dark mood. She punched her pillow. She was tired, but she wasn't sleepy.

Someone knocked at her door. "El?" It was Jack.

"What?"

"We're going to do chores, but we'll see if you wanna go before we leave. Okay?" It was an apology. For Jack.

"Fine."

Eleanor lay for a long time, stewing. She couldn't hear anything, but after a while she knew the house was empty. She got under the covers, and their weight made her feel better, and sleepy. She drifted off.

Bright sunlight showed around the edges of the shades. Eleanor wasn't sure what woke her, but a door shut somewhere in the house. They must have finished chores. She stretched, surprised she had no aches or pains from last night.

Something had sorted itself out while she slept. She was no longer angry. Being *aware* of the Realm actually was cool, contrary to what she'd yelled at Jack. She wasn't sure why she'd been so angry. Maybe she'd been picking up Jack's irritation.

Eleanor lay, thinking. No, the Realm wasn't a threat, but there *was* a threat. Something was attracting Noctivagi to the area, and with the location of the Chalice unknown … it had to be the Chalice. It needed to be found and returned it to the Undine Prince.

Doris didn't have it—that was obvious—and the only one who ever entered her cave was Nob.

Nob!

Eleanor sat straight up. Nob had something to do with this. Somehow she knew it. She jumped out of bed and pulled on her jeans. She grabbed the sheath of knives under her pillow and slid it onto her belt. Jack wanted in? Eleanor smiled. He might regret saying that.

Chapter Sixteen

She thundered down the stairs, yelling, "Guys! Hey guys!"

Rob poked his head out the swinging kitchen door. "Where's the fire?"

She strode to the kitchen. They were sitting around the table, eating lunch. "Come on, we're going riding."

"Feeling better, Sybil?" asked Jack.

"Yes, much," she said.

"What's gotten into you?"

"We need to find Nob. We'll check the dam. Even if he isn't there, Meg might be and know where he is."

"Why?" Rob asked.

"He's involved in this, somehow. He knows something he isn't sharing. Either about the Chalice, or Doris—there's a missing piece here and it has to do with him."

"Couldn't be a Pyske, could it?" Jack raised an eyebrow. "Nooo, the Sea Dragon is key."

"Can we eat first?" Rob asked.

"Yeah." Eleanor got the bread and sandwich meat.

"I still don't get why you are all fired up all of a sudden," Jack said.

"I've had my last dead body land on me."

"Geez, El," Rob said, glancing at Flora.

"You know what? Flora can handle it. Can't you, Florie?"

Flora nodded, eyes big.

"Protecting her isn't keeping her safe. She's seen the monster. She knows what it is. What they are. She needs to learn to defend herself, just like us. Finish up. Let's go."

They put their dishes in the sink, left a note for Mrs. Bradford, and headed to the barn.

The horses were in the pasture, and all was quiet.

"Where are the Pyskes?"

"Apparently they don't like the hot noonday sun. They *siesta*," Jack said, amused.

"Really?"

"Yep. Felix hovered this morning while we were cleaning the stalls, and talked the entire time. We know all about Pyskes now. Ever wondered?" Jack snorted. "They prefer gathering pollen with dew, so they're morning and evening gatherers. Furthermore, the sun dries their wings out, which is irritating, so they sleep during the noon hours. Patters, by the way, is threatening to move out."

They grabbed the bridles, got the horses and left. The Elves Handrven and Maethoron materialized beside the trail to the Lee. "Where are you headed?"

"For a swim. Where is Baelhar?"

"Busy," Handrven said. It was the most Eleanor had ever heard him say. The bored look on his face indicated he didn't enjoy guard duty any more than the kids did.

They cut through the park and made it to the dam in short order.

There was no sign of Meg. Eleanor leaned forward on Ginger's withers and scanned the riverbanks. She shook her head, disappointed. She slid from Gingers back and sat on a rock to remove her boots and jeans.

"What are you doing?" asked Jack.

"I'm going swimming. Maybe she'll hear us."

"In your tee shirt?"

"A little credit. I have my bathing suit on," she said. She peeled her shirt off.

"You know, El," Rob said. "Maybe we should wait."

"Why?"

"Well, Nob …"

"Nob's the one I'm looking for," she said. Seeing the uncertainty on his face she added, "Don't worry, Rob. We're in no danger from Nob."

Eleanor waded into the river and dove. She surfaced, treading water and looking around. She swam for the other bank. Rob slid off Sargent's back and began removing his clothes.

"Where are you going?" asked Jack.

"I can't very well let her swim out there alone," he said. "Stay with Flora."

"Dun dun daaaaa. It's a bird. It's a plane. It's Boxer Man! To the rescue!" Jack sang.

Rob ignored him and followed Eleanor into the water.

Handrven and Maethoron appeared.

"What is she doing?" Maethoron asked.

"Looking for Nob," Jack informed him, waiting for the reaction.

He wasn't disappointed.

"She … she shouldn't be doing that!" Handrven started for the river.

"She's fine," Jack said. He slid from Ringo's back and walked to the river's edge, watching.

"She's not fine! She has no business—"

"What's going on?" Gunnr walked from the woods.

"Eleanor went for a little swim," Jack said. "She's looking for Nob."

Gunnr walked to a granite boulder beside the river and sat. *"What are you doing?"*

"Hang on." Eleanor swam farther downriver, searching under the water, Rob in her wake.

"Come on back, Eleanor."

"No, I want to find Nob."

"You know, I don't believe anyone's ever uttered those words."

"He knows something about the Chalice."

"Why do you say that?"

"I just have a feeling."

Handrven walked over to Gunnr, an annoyed look on his face. "Since you're here, we'll be leaving."

Gunnr kept his eye on Eleanor and Rob in the river, but said, "You have guard today?"

"Yes."

"Then you'll stay, and guard them until you are relieved."

"And babysit? This is ridiculous—"

Gunnr turned so fast Handrven took a step back.

Maethoron quickly stepped between the two, his hands up. "We'll stay with them."

Handrven's eyes flashed, but he held his tongue.

The tension between the two Elves was palpable.

Gunnr said, "We need to be able to trust—"

"You're one to lecture about trust," Handrven spat.

Gunnr smiled, but Jack saw a muscle in his jaw ticking. Handrven must have seen it as well. He shut up.

"As I was saying," Gunnr continued. "Whoever is guarding these children must be dedicated to the task." His tone hardened. "There are Noctivagi in the area. There've been six deaths

in two days."

The Elf sneered. "Noctivagi can't walk in the sun."

From the look on Gunnr's face, it was obvious he thought Handrven was a fool. "These children will be supervised and accompanied. *At all times.*"

Handrven glared at Gunnr. Jack felt power crackle in the air as the two faced each other.

"Yes or no?" Gunnr's quiet tone was far more menacing the Handrven's bluster.

Finally, the guard looked away and muttered, "Yes."

"Well, now that that's settled," Meg said, walking from the river. Rob and Eleanor followed, Mim and Vidia behind them. "No one mentioned a party."

Jack gasped when he saw the other two Water Sprites, and it broke the tension between Gunnr and Handrven.

Eleanor wrung the water from her ponytail. "Nob's not here. Meg said she hasn't seen him since we were here the other day."

"He was in the harbor yesterday, El," Jack reminded her. "Told you we should have taken the boat."

"We might as well," Eleanor said.

"We'll watch for him in the river," Meg offered.

Rob struggled to pull his jeans on as they stuck to his wet legs. "We can check in the harbor. I don't know how we're going to find him, though, if he doesn't want to be found."

"I'm not sure he's hiding," Eleanor said.

"Look, let's ride back, and then we can check the harbor tomorrow," Jack said. "We'll take the whaler."

"Why not today?" Eleanor asked.

"Not enough time, El. By the time we get back to the barn, it'll be time to clean up for dinner. You'll need it. Wait until you see yourself."

Eleanor opened her mouth to argue and caught the look on Jack's face. He had something in mind.

"Fine. We can check tomorrow. Thanks, Meg. Vidia, Mim."

Meg and Mim smiled. Vidia gave her a cold look and walked back into the river.

They led the horses along the path. Eleanor and Rob, in stiff, wet jeans, looked for a rock they could use to help mount their horses.

Gunnr realized the problem and smiled. "Leg up?" he offered Rob.

"Thanks."

Eleanor placed her hand holding the reins on Ginger's withers, and facing the horse, bent her leg for a boost, too. Once settled on the horse's back, she asked Gunnr, "No lesson today, right?"

"No. I have something I have to do. You guys can set up a target in the barn and practice throwing if you want. Same time tomorrow, though." He eyed the Elves. "So I trust you'll follow them home." It wasn't a question.

Handrven frowned, but nodded.

"Very good," he gave Ginger's flank a pat. His outline blurred, and he disappeared.

Eleanor closed the pasture gate and went into the barn. "So what was that all about? We have plenty of time to check around the harbor."

"Have you noticed where the Elves wait?" asked Jack.

"Yeah, by the Lee ... ahhh," she said, putting it together. "No guards if we go by boat. Unless they know."

"Bingo! She can be taught! They didn't follow us to Lime last time because they didn't know. They guard the road."

"You actually are smarter than you look, Jack. I don't really care about the guards, though."

"I don't need a babysitter. And you missed the confrontation on the riverbank before you swam in. I thought Gunnr was going to tear Handrven apart. There's some history there."

"Eh, whatever. We better hurry."

"I need to change before we go," Rob said. His gait was stiff.

"Don't get your panties in a bunch," Jack said, and then laughed, delighted with his own joke. "Why didn't you just take your wet boxers off?"

"In front of everyone? Yeah. Sure." Rob snorted.

"Hey, I didn't tell you to dive in," Eleanor said.

They entered the house. "Let's just change, okay? We don't have a lot of time."

"Five minutes."

Eleanor peeled off her wet jeans, tossed them in the tub, and pulled cutoffs on over her bathing suit. She fed the belt through the loops at her hips, adjusting the position of the small leather sheath. She liked the knives. Wished she'd had them when Eilvain attacked. Grabbing flip-slops and a sweatshirt, she ran back downstairs, meeting Rob on the landing.

They headed to the dock. Jack and Flora retrieved their life vests from the boathouse while Rob and Eleanor pulled the whaler in on the outhaul.

Eleanor took the stern and started the outboard. Surprisingly, neither Rob nor Jack argued. "Let's check the lighthouse first. Maybe Seaton knows something."

The tide was high, and Eleanor cut straight to the rocks surrounding the small island. They circled the island slowly, searching for the seal, but he wasn't there. Eleanor idled the engine and stood, scanning the harbor and beyond, wondering where else he might be.

"Try there." Jack pointed beyond the mouth of the harbor. A metal tower and reflective sign warned mariners away from the ledges to which it was mounted.

Large gray bodies covered those ledges, sunning themselves.

Eleanor reached to put the boat in gear and paused, listening. She turned to Rob and Jack, and they had the same odd looks on their faces. Just discernible over the low thrum of the engine, another sound reached across the water. Eleanor shut the engine off and they listened.

Well it's all for me grog,
me jolly jolly grog

It's all for me beer
and tobacco

Flora asked, "Are those seals … *singing?*"

I spent all me loot
in a house of ill repute

Jack was delighted. "*Awesome.*"

Rob grinned. "So seals don't bark, after all."

And I think I'll have to go
back there tommmmor - row.

"A raunchy pirate song. Cool. So that's why they're called sea *dogs.*"

Eleanor rolled her eyes, engaged the whaler, and headed over.

Round heads lifted at their approach, curious. Eleanor cut the engine to low and nosed closer. The seals stopped singing. Some of the more skittish ones slid into the water and swam away. The larger seals stayed, watching the boat, but unconcerned.

"Seaton around?"

Every seal remaining lifted its head, shocked to understand Rob's question.

"Who wantth to know?" the largest seal asked with a lisp.

"Anyone seen him?" Rob pushed.

"Did you check the Lighthouth?"

"Yes."

"Can't help you, then, mate. But if we thee him, we'll tell 'im you're looking."

"Thanks."

Eleanor put the outboard in reverse and backed off the rocks. She looked at her sister and brothers. "Now what?"

"Hey!" Rob hollered back to the seal.

"Yeth?"

"You haven't seen Nob, have you?"

The seal shuddered, the blubber on him rolling like a wave. "Try Lime. He hangth with Dorith."

"Thanks!"

"Righto, Mate. Luck."

Eleanor looked across to the island, judging the chop on the bay. "It's not bad. We can take this over without having our teeth rattled out of our heads."

"Think we have time?" Rob asked. The sun was sinking in the afternoon sky.

"We have time. Go for it, but swing low, by The Graves, before you head over," Jack said.

"Why?"

"Might see something. Good place for seals."

"Or bodies," Eleanor said, under her breath.

Jack scoffed. "Don't be such a baby."

"I've never seen seals there. It isn't a *seal* place. It's a shark place."

"Hurry up, El. We don't have all day."

Eleanor looked to Rob, who shrugged, and she turned south. She slowed the small boat as they neared the jagged ledges. The waves churned, tugging the craft to a smashed and splintered end, but Eleanor held the whaler steady as she circled the treacherous cropping. Her white knuckles clenched the tiller handle's twist grip against the pull—or maybe the stories of The Graves were getting to her. Eleanor wanted to leave this place. She was relieved to see no sign of life. Nothing stirred. Not even seabirds lingered in the forsaken spot.

Eleanor turned the boat toward Lime. The bay was calm and the whaler skated across the water's flat surface in minutes, but even as they left the craggy expanse behind them, the uneasy feeling stayed with Eleanor.

"Try Little Bermuda, too," Rob said.

"Between Job and Lime?"

Rob nodded, shading his eyes, trying to see the spot.

She slowed on her approach to Little Bermuda, circling the rock.

Rob pointed. A large gray body lay on one of the lower ledges, tail up in the air. She pulled closer.

"Hel-lo," Rob called.

"Well, right. Driscolls to port. How're yer seas?"

"Fine, Seaton. We're looking for Nob. You haven't seen him, have you?"

"What you want him fer?" the seal asked.

"I have a few questions for him, is all," Eleanor said.

His tail dropped, and he looked around. He slid to a rock

below him. "'Bout what?" Seaton asked in a lower voice.

Eleanor realized old Seaton was sharper than he let on.

"A couple questions, that's all."

"You'd be smart to stay away from the Midgard Serpent. He's an ugly git—"

The Dragon's large golden head broke the surface beside the boat. "It's fine, Seaton. I knew someone would be along eventually. Though this lot is a surprise." Rivulets of water ran down his snout and dripped off his horns. He tilted his head and asked the kids, "You know, don't you?"

Chapter Seventeen

"You have it, don't you?" Eleanor said.

"You could say that."

"Where is it?"

"It's not prudent to discuss here. We should go to Doris's cave."

Jack laughed, incredulous. "Yeah, right."

Eleanor reached to put the whaler back in gear, but Jack stayed her arm. "Have you lost your mind? You're going into an underground cavern with a Sea Dragon? Really?"

Nob snorted, blowing water droplets into the air.

"Jack, we have to talk to him," Eleanor said.

"No, we don't. Tell Camedon."

"Camedon isn't here. We are."

"You're out of your mind. And, it's getting late. We're losing our daylight."

"We have plenty of time, but only if we get on this." Eleanor turned to Nob. "Lead the way." She put the whaler in gear and followed the Dragon toward Lime Island.

Rob tried reason. "We can't enter that cavern, El. We have no way to get out."

"I'll go. You wait with the whaler. He might change his mind. We need to get the Chalice to Camedon."

"Call Gunnr. Camedon could be here in a minute."

"He might not give it to Camedon, but I think he'll give it

to me. Look, you guys. We have nothing to lose. Just let me try. We can always leave." Eleanor beached the skiff, and hopped out.

"This is a *really* bad idea, El," Rob insisted.

"I've got a good feeling about it. Trust me."

She walked to the rock entrance of Doris' cavern. The scope of the Dragon's great body showed in the shallow water and Eleanor knew a moment of uncertainty. "I'm not entering the cavern with you."

He blinked his golden eyes, taking her measure. "I suppose I understand your reluctance."

"I'm not worried about you. It's Doris who scares me."

His eyes crinkled at the corners. "I've learned a few things about you. I wouldn't think, after a Noctivagus, a Water Witch would bother you."

"Where *is* Doris?"

"I have no idea. She may even be in her cavern, but I don't think so."

Rob, Jack, and Flora approached.

"In for a penny, in for a pound, as they say," Rob said.

"No one says that," Jack muttered.

Nob dismissed them, returning his attention to Eleanor. "We needn't go in the cavern, but I won't sit here drying out, either. The sun has dropped, but the shade is more comfortable. Follow me."

He rose from the water, and Eleanor was surprised to see he had legs. She'd imagined a serpentine body below the water's surface.

The sun's dying rays glinted on his golden scales, and the Dragon was radiant. He lumbered across the beach, his great tail furrowing the sand in his wake. Thick claws gouged the sand with each step. The kids followed, but not closely, as he crossed the beach and entered the trees. He didn't stop, but headed farther in to the island's center.

The worn track and gouges in the dirt revealed he'd traveled this way before. He finally came to rest against the crumbling foundation of one of the abandoned houses, and settled his great body into a worn depression.

"Do you live here?"

"Sometimes I sleep here," he said. His words were one long rumble and Eleanor had to pay attention to understand him.

Eleanor cut to the chase. "Tell me about the Chalice."

"What about it?"

His head was massive, the size of Eleanor's body, and when he returned his attention to her the movement reminded her how vulnerable they really were. She tamped down her unease. "Why did you take it?"

"Doris should have left it where it sank. It was safe on the ocean floor."

Jack snorted. "I would have guessed it was pretty safe in her cave, too."

"It's quite safe where it is now." The Dragon gave a bitter laugh, and the granite blocks he leaned against trembled.

"Where is it?" Eleanor asked, completely unprepared for his answer.

"In the belly of the beast."

"What?"

"I swallowed it." Though it was hard to tell with a Dragon, Eleanor thought he looked proud of himself.

"Why did you do that?" Rob asked.

"Seemed like a good idea at the time."

"Seriously, dude," Jack said, stepping closer. The Dragon turned his head to him, and Jack stilled. "Seriously," he said in a softer voice.

"It wasn't safe with Doris. She is so … irrational about Newlin, who knows what she may have decided to do with it. Distraught, angry, vindictive, and sometimes all three in as many minutes. Never understood. The milksop wasn't worthy of her affections. Obviously." He paused. "That being said, the Chalice is too important to be in the hands of someone so emotionally fragile."

A voice thundered behind them. "Emotionally fragile? Emotionally *fragile*! I'll show you emotionally fragile! How dare you remove that from my cavern!"

Doris strode toward them with fiber in her step and fire in her ugly, bulging eyes.

"What happened to her tail?" Jack whispered.

Eleanor shrugged. "She's a witch."

"You know I'm right, Doris," Nob said, not at all repentant.

Her eyes popped even farther. "Emotionally *fragile*?"

"Looked in the mirror, Luv? Your appearance doesn't lend itself to mental stability."

"How dare you!" She raised her thick, scaly arms toward the skies, and energy crackled around her. Her hair stood straight out. She seemed to grow taller. A loud *crack* split the air.

Before them stood an entirely different Being. The kids gasped at her transformation.

Doris the Fair stood where Doris the Water Witch had stood a moment before. Tall and statuesque in clinging robes, her face captivated, even flushed with anger. Thick locks of hair flowed down her back in gold and bronze waves. Her eyes, though, were the most dramatic change. What had been a creepy, clouded opalescent color now could only be described as a brilliant green. They flashed with anger.

"Ah, there she is. Been missing you, Luv." The Dragon's rumble sounded like a contented cat's purr.

"What are you playing at, Nob? You had *no* right—"

"I most certainly had a right," the Dragon cut her off. "I had a duty. To the Chalice, to you, to the Realm, and to the waters."

"The Alabaster Chalice was perfectly safe in my possession."

"Then how did I take it so easily? You never even noticed its absence."

"Why would I? I trusted you. You were the *only* one I trusted in my cavern. Give it back to me!"

"No."

The witch took step closer. "Nob!"

The tension between the Witch and the Dragon thickened. Energy crackled in the air. Eleanor was swamped with feelings of anger, sadness, and loss radiating from both of them, but another feeling crept in. Eleanor couldn't identify the source, but it was insidious. She backed a few steps from the two, herding her brothers and sister with her.

The feeling was not coming from the Dragon. He was matter-of-fact when he said to Doris, "No, I will give it to Camedon. He may decide whether Newlin should retain charge of the artifact." His tone was final, leaving no room for argument, but he softened it, and added. "No one is more special to me, Doris, but the Alabaster Chalice does not belong with you. It is a sacred relic, representing one of the four Elements. Whether Newlin's carelessness cost him the honor of guarding the Chalice, well, only Camedon can make that decision."

"Foolishness, but do with it what you will. I don't care about the Chalice. I do care that you took it!"

The evil grew, and Eleanor's skin crawled at the foul darkness. She'd only felt it once before. Realization dawned as the smell of rotting flesh filled the air. Eleanor dropped to her knees and gagged.

Reeling in the malevolence descending around them, Eleanor looked up as four foul creatures materialized.

"*We* care about the Chalice," snarled the Noctivagus.

Eleanor's skin crawled at the evil silk of his voice.

"Give it here."

Chapter Eighteen

THOUGH SHE WOULDN'T HAVE THOUGHT IT POSSIBLE, THE Noctivagi before them were even more grotesque than Eilvain. Decaying gray skin sagged on partially exposed, wizened skulls. Their hands were bony claws, nails yellowed and coarse. Straggles of long hair hung from scaly, rotting patches of scalp.

Eleanor swallowed shallow breaths through her mouth but the stench invaded. Oppressive evil permeated the air. The monsters amplified hopelessness and despair. Waves of misery rolled over her, leaving her shaky. Eleanor clenched her teeth and imagined a physical wall protecting her from the foul assault, thick and strong. She threw her hand up, as to reinforce the wall, and stood on weak, shaky legs.

Jack shoved Flora behind him, "Stay down," he hissed and stepped in front of her.

"Now might be a good time to call Camedon," Rob said to Eleanor out of the side of his mouth.

One of the monsters sneered. "We know the Keeper isn't here," it gloated. "Get on the ground. Don't move." Eleanor recognized the compulsion in his voice, even as Rob, Jack, and Flora fell to their knees. Though Eleanor could resist the compulsion, she didn't want to draw attention to herself. She knelt, and reached for Gunnr.

"We're being attacked by four Noctivagi."

"Where?" he asked, his voice flat and dangerous.

One of the Noctivagi looked around, eyes narrowed as if he sensed something.

Eleanor kept her expression blank. *"Lime Island. In the middle, by the foundations. Nob is here, and he has the Chalice. Doris is too. They were arguing and the Noctivagi appeared. I don't know how much they overheard."*

"Don't do anything to draw their attention to you. Look afraid."

"That won't be a problem."

Before she'd finished the thought, Gunnr and Camedon materialized between the kids and the Noctivagi.

Immediately, a shield of protection surrounded Eleanor and her brothers and sister.

Moments later Baelhar, Handrven, and Maethoron appeared beside them.

"Ahhh, the cavalry," one of the Noctivagi said, a twisted parody of a smile stretching across his face.

"Radek," Gunnr greeted the monster casually. "We appreciate you coming to receive final justice. Saves us a trip."

"You! How dare you address me."

Gunnr's smile sent chills down Eleanor's spine. "And you brought friends. Jurim, Gustav, and Bryce. Company in the afterlife. How nice for you, Radek."

The Noctivagus hissed and stepped toward Gunnr, but Eleanor felt a new emotion swirling about the soulless monsters. Fear. Rancid fear soured the air.

Eleanor looked for Doris and saw Nob had positioned himself between the Witch and the Noctivagi.

Radek postured. "You sniveling coward! You spend your existence clinging to a half-life. For what? To serve those who will never accept you? Those who could never appreciate the raw power you wield, but instead keep you leashed like a dog?" Radek spat.

"Don't make eye contact with any of them. Tell Rob, Jack, and Flora. Keep Flora behind you. Radek is old and powerful. Evil beyond your imagining. Being outnumbered will only make him desperate and more dangerous. He's not above anything to escape this situation unscathed. Don't look at them."

Eleanor caught movement behind Radek. The three Noctivagi were sidling backwards.

"Watch them!"

Camedon must have seen it, too, because he stepped forward and asked, "What brings you out of hiding, Radek? Why are you revealing yourself to those who would impose the death sentence on your head? Do you seek eternal rest? Has the filth of your soul become too great a burden?"

The Noctivagus scoffed. "Your ineptitude has enabled us to seize one of the artifacts and control an element."

"Mmm, it would appear so, wouldn't it? I wonder, though, why you think you will be allowed to leave with it. You'll have to get by four Warriors of the Realm, a Keeper, a Dragon, and a Witch," Camedon said.

Camedon's goading had the desired result, spurring a reaction from Radek. He snapped his teeth menacingly and drool oozed from his mouth. His head undulated back and forth on his shoulders in a macabre rhythm, reminding Eleanor of a snake hypnotizing its victim.

The other three Noctivagi spread out. Jurim raised his hands and threw a ball of fire at an old spruce tree, knocking it down with a crash.

The battle exploded.

Handrven went after Jurim, who leapt onto the foundation

wall and dropped another tree between them. He raised his hands and the wind increased, fanning the flames.

Baelhar drew his sword and charged the Noctivagus, Bryce, who blocked the sword's strike and raked his talons across Baelhar's arm.

Maethoron backed Gustav toward the woods. The Noctivagi lifted his hands, summoning a tangle of tree roots from the ground to entwine Maethoron's legs. Maethoron burned the creeping roots to ash with a wave of his hand, but the roots continued to come from the ground and block his progress.

Doris's lips moved, an intense expression on her face as she incanted. Doris swept her hands wide. Water bubbled from the ground. The earth under each Noctivagus became wet and soupy and they lost their footing and stumbled.

Bryce launched himself skyward to escape the muck, and Baelhar followed him, grabbed his leg, and hurtled back to the earth.

When Jurim faltered, Handrven struck what should have been a killing blow, but Jurim avoided it by dissolving to mist, and falling to the puddle. Handrven formed a ball of white fire in his hands and reduced the puddle to steam in a flash of light. A scream rent the air and Jurim regained his shape a few feet away, scorched and smoking.

Eleanor was relieved Flora was behind them. Though Flora couldn't see, Eleanor knew the sounds of the battle must be terrifying, and she held her sister's hand tightly. Jack and Rob were mesmerized by the fighting.

Nob backed steadily toward the woods, pushing Doris back, keeping his massive golden body between her and the battle. His tail slashed, and he roared. Eleanor expected flames, but none came.

The sound was like thunder, and the Noctivagus Gustav was distracted just long enough for Maethoron to sink his sword through his chest. Maethoron thrust hard and pinned the struggling Noctivagus to the ground. He pulled energy from the skies, growing a great ball of light in his hands, and shouted over the din of the battle, "As a Warrior of the Realm, I deliver your death sentence. May your soul find peace in the next life." He threw the ball of white light and incinerated the Noctivagus still squirming on the sword. As the body turned to ash, the sword fell to the ground.

Maethoron turned to help Gunnr, but Gunnr waved him off. "Get the others."

Maethoron tossed him his sword. Gunnr caught it and advanced on Radek, forcing him backward toward Nob. Radek lunged, but Gunnr sidestepped his assault and laid the Noctivagus' back wide open. Radek hissed in pain and stumbled. He recovered and spun, kicking Gunnr's feet from under him. Radek seized the advantage and jumped on him, slashing at Gunnr's neck with his clawed hands. Gunnr threw him over his head and came to his feet. He towered over Radek, sword high, when Radek remembered the kids.

"That one is special. Feels things, doesn't she?" The malicious smile on his face grew.

Crippling pain struck Eleanor, and she cried out. The monster forced hopelessness, misery, and fear into her mind. Trying to escape the maniacal laughter, she gripped her head.

She felt Gunnr take control and fight back, throwing up barriers, placing himself between her and Radek's invasion. He sought to absorb the pain and misery, but still, Eleanor doubled over in agony.

Radek withdrew from Eleanor's mind as fast as he'd invaded.

She lay on the ground, gasping, ashen and clammy.

Radek jumped to his feet, drawing his own sword. He leapt into the air, and before anyone could stop him, he swung at Nob's neck and sliced his head clean off.

Doris' scream filled the air. Everyone froze, watching Radek in horror.

The next slash of the sword laid Nob's belly open. Radek reached in and pulled the Chalice from the Dragon's steaming innards.

Snatching the Dragon's massive head from the ground, Radek held it and the Chalice over his head. An evil, triumphant smile grew on his face. "See here, Keeper? See here!" Radek shook the Chalice and the Dragon's head, spraying blood everywhere.

Doris shrieked and launched at the Noctivagus in a grief-stricken, killing fury. Handrven grabbed her before she could reach Radek. He pinned her to the ground as she sobbed.

Radek laughed. "Sell his scales, Doris, you'll make a fortune." He threw the head at her. It landed and rolled, leaving a trail of blood.

Eleanor retched. She prayed Flora couldn't see.

"You aren't leaving here alive, Radek," Gunnr said in a threat so low it was almost a growl. "You know that." He threw three knives in rapid succession into the Noctivagus's chest, impaling his heart. Radek bellowed, ripped the knives out, and charged.

Baelhar sent a path of flames across the ground toward Bryce. When Bryce fled to the skies, Maethoron was waiting and tackled him. They both crashed back to the ground. Baelhar stood, a great ball of hot, white energy in his hands, and incinerated Bryce the moment his body stopped rolling.

They did not pause, but went after the Noctivagus Jurim, who'd been so intent on sneaking up behind Camedon that he hadn't seen Bryce fall. When the Warriors landed on either side of him, he was caught off guard. He lashed out, but it was too little, too late. Baelhar took him down, and Maethoron delivered justice in a lethal, burning ball. He sent it straight through the Noctivagus, leaving a hole through its chest. A moment later, the rest of the monster's body incinerated to ash.

Camedon moved to Doris and dropped to the ground beside her. Eleanor could not hear what the Keeper said, but Doris lifted her tear-stained face and listened. She pulled herself to her feet, and shaking off Camedon's hand she went to the Dragon's head. She lifted it, and cradling it gently, carried it to the neck of the body. She knelt and placed it so it appeared attached.

Gunnr and Radek faced each other, sides heaving. Blood streamed from the deep cut in Gunnr's thigh. Radek was a mess of blood and gaping wounds. They'd thrown the swords to the side. Radek was at a disadvantage, unable to use the arm in which he clutched the Chalice. Baelhar, Maethoron, and Handrven landed, surrounding him and preventing his escape.

A plaintive wail brought everyone's attention back to Doris. She sunk to her knees beside Nob. All watched, horrified, as the body of the great Dragon smoldered and began to change, twisting and shrinking. After a moment the Dragon was gone, and another body took its place, head intact. A man.

Snatching the Dragon's massive head from the ground, he held it and the Chalice over his head, an evil, triumphant smile on his face.

Chapter Nineteen

NEWLIN, THE UNDINE PRINCE, LAY ON THE GROUND IN FRONT of Doris.

Doris's agony pierced the ears and the hearts of those who heard it. She threw herself on his corpse, sobbing and rocking.

Camedon and the warriors stared at the body, dumbstruck. Eleanor thought of the golden eyes and couldn't believe she hadn't put it together.

Doris's grief rolled through Eleanor anew, but she shoved it out, forcefully, more concerned with Radek. She suspected he'd seize the opportunity afforded him, and he did, gathering himself to strike.

"Watch him," she yelled, afraid he'd attack Gunnr.

Radek was fast, but escape was what he sought, and he launched himself, fleeing to the skies.

The warriors made to pursue, but Camedon stopped them. "Let him go," he said, weariness in his voice.

"He has the Chalice. We can catch him," Baelhar argued.

Camedon shook his head. "He can't go far. He's gravely wounded. He'll go to ground. We'll have no problem finding him. His blood marks a toxic trail." The spatters of noxious substance on the ground steamed. He waved his hand and incinerated every visible trace, then went to Doris.

Gunnr straightened and walked to the kids, holding the wound on his leg. He waved his hand and removed the protective shield he'd thrown over them. As it dropped, Doris' grief overwhelmed Eleanor. She realized the shield had protected against some of the emotion swirling, and wondered how agonizing Radek's attack might have been without the protections in place.

Jack and Rob allowed Flora to step forward, and Gunnr knelt before her. "Are you all right?"

She nodded, eyes large.

"She couldn't see much," Rob said.

"Still, the sounds alone would have been terrifying. You were very, very brave, Flora. I'm proud of you." Gunnr gave Flora's shoulder a squeeze. He looked at Eleanor. "*All right?*"

She nodded. "*What was that?*"

"*Radek is ruthless. He sensed your abilities and used it against us.*"

"*How do I defend against that?*"

"*You already are, to some extent—you did several times without even realizing. But we'll practice, strengthen your defenses. I'm proud of you.*" Approval showed warm in his eyes.

Eleanor took her sweatshirt and handed it to him, indicating the blood still running down his leg. He didn't take it, but drew a line of white *heiling* light over the gaping wound, and it closed.

"What are they doing?" asked Jack, jerking his head toward the Elven Guards.

"They are looking for tainted debris from the Noctivagi. Even in death, they're dangerous. They must be completely destroyed. Their blood is toxic. Their flesh will consume what it touches."

Trees were uprooted, and acrid smoke stung throats. Destruction littered the area. Everyone averted their attention from Doris, covered in blood, stroking Newlin's hair.

Camedon stood behind her, head bowed. After a few moments, he took her gently by the shoulders, attempting to guide her away, but she shook him off, sobbing quietly.

The Keeper stepped back, allowing her more time. Grief evident on his face, he bowed his head again, and stood quietly behind her.

Her keening stopped suddenly with a gasp, and she lurched back, making Camedon falter.

Newlin's arm twitched, then his body spasmed, arching off the ground. It twisted and writhed, just as it had done a few moments before, except this time he emitted groans and gasps.

Gunnr threw a protective shield back over the kids. The warriors drew their swords, and Camedon pulled Doris back.

Energy crackled around the body in flashes and arcs, and then stilled, leaving it limp and motionless on the ground.

No one moved, and when Newlin's eyes opened, Doris collapsed in a dead faint.

The Undine Prince lay motionless for several moments, and then sat up and wheezed, "Can't say I care to do that again."

Baelhar was the first to find his voice. "What was that?"

"*That* was the power of the Alabaster Chalice." Camedon offered his hand to the prince and pulled him to his feet. "Wasn't it?"

The prince moved to Doris and knelt beside her. "Yes. Although, I don't understand. Radek must have severed my head with that blow. I never saw it coming."

"He did. Completely. But Doris laid it back at Nob's neck."

"The two pieces must have touched. The Chalice restores life, but only if the body is intact."

"You've drunk from the Chalice?"

"Yes."

Doris stirred, and Newlin cradled her head. She opened her

eyes, dazed.

"I don't understand." She cupped his face in her palm. "How …?"

"It was the only way I could appease the Undine until I was crowned as King. Forgive me, Doris."

She sat up and gazed at him, but after a few moments a frown replaced her relief. "All these years … all these *years*! And you never said anything!" She stood, her anger growing as she realized, as she remembered. "How dare you!"

"I rather think you've asked me that enough today, Luv," he said, his smile apologetic.

Doris slapped his face and spun, stalking toward her cavern, hair streaming behind her.

"I think she's mad, Newlin," Baelhar said.

"She often is," he said, his gaze following her. He sighed and turned back to Camedon. "Where *is* the Chalice?"

"Radek managed to escape with it," Camedon said.

Newlin stood, alarmed. "We need to find him!"

"It shouldn't be hard," Camedon assured the prince. "He was injured."

Gunnr's head snapped up. "What if he drinks from it, too? He'll recover and we'll never find him. Or it."

"He won't." Camedon turned to the warriors. "Go while his trail is fresh. I'll take care of things here."

Baelhar, Maethoron, and Handrven dissolved in thin air.

Gunnr looked to Newlin. "Can Nob be resurrected? To help Camedon escort the kids home?"

Newlin nodded, but by his frown Eleanor surmised he'd rather hunt for the Noctivagus and the Chalice with the warriors.

Gunnr and Eleanor's eyes met as his form blurred and disappeared.

"*When you find him,*" she said, "*sever his head before you incinerate the body. Just in case.*"

Gunnr's chuckle echoed in her mind. "*I always forget what a bloodthirsty little thing you are.*"

"Well then," Camedon said, looking around. "Do need to see Doris before we leave?" he asked Newlin.

The Undine Prince shook his head. "Best give her a little time to cool off. Lots of sharp things in her cavern."

"Hey. Maybe one of you could remove the bubble?" Jack said.

Camedon removed it with a wave of his hand, and they headed for beach.

Newlin entered the water. A glow of golden light surrounded his body as he transformed into the Dragon. He waited in the shallows while Rob and Jack slid the whaler into the water.

Camedon stepped in and found his seat in the bow.

"You're going?" asked Jack.

"Lovely evening for a boat ride."

Eleanor lifted Flora and passed her to Camedon before hoisting herself over the side of the whaler. Rob and Jack jumped in, and Rob took control of the outboard.

The bay was calm and the whaler crossed in minutes. Nob swam off its starboard bow. Jack kept his eye on Camedon, hoping to at least discern a tinge of green on his cheeks, but the Keeper seemed to enjoy the boat ride. It wasn't completely dark, but mast lights in the harbor twinkled like low-hanging stars.

Rob slid the whaler along the float. Jack hopped out and tied the bow and stern lines.

The Dragon rested his head on the float and asked, "All set?"

"Yes," Camedon said, levitating to the dock.

Flora giggled at the Keeper's magic, and Eleanor appreciated his attempt at levity. Levitate? Levity? She almost laughed aloud.

Camedon winked at her. Did he know what she was thinking? He grinned. He did!

"Good night, then." The Dragon blinked a large golden eye and sunk below the surface of the water.

"Come now," Camedon said. "Let's check on Charlotte." He guided Flora up the incline. Rob, Jack, and Eleanor followed. Though the point was safeguarded with ancient protections, Rob and Jack peered into the shadows nervously. Eleanor couldn't blame them, but she didn't bother. She wouldn't fail to recognize the evil disturbance the Noctivagi caused again. They were unnatural, and nature recoiled in their presence.

The house was brightly lit, and Charlotte and Agnes met them on the terrace.

"Thank you for sending Agnes, Camedon. I would have worried."

"You were worried anyway," Agnes said. She flew to Eleanor's shoulder and pecked her ear.

"Ow! What was that for?"

"Stupidity," the crow said. "Didn't I tell you to look sharp? That trouble was upon us?" The crow ruffled her feathers and settled on Eleanor's shoulder. She was heavy, but Eleanor suffered the weight rather than risk another peck.

"Why don't you peck Jack?" Eleanor muttered.

"All's well that ends well," Charlotte said.

"We hope. They've gone after Radek," Camedon told the librarian.

"Dinner is served, Madam," a voice announced, properly.

Floyd stood in the doorway. He was formally attired in a somber black suit, his hair slicked back. He stood stiffly, not making eye contact, but addressing something over their heads.

"Thank you, Floyd," Charlotte answered. "We'll be right in."

"Might I suggest we forgo dressing for dinner this evening, in the interest of time? Perhaps the young masters and misses could instead freshen themselves in the downstairs powder room?"

"Yes, Floyd, I think that's a practical suggestion," Charlotte said, benignly.

"Very good, Madam." The Hob left the room.

"What's that all about?" asked Jack.

"Floyd is settling in," Charlotte explained. "Black Ledge always had a Hob in attendance. So nice to have one again."

"He was in the barn before. What's the deal with the butler stuff?" asked Jack.

"Hobs oversee everything. They aren't housebound like other Beings, but manage entire properties. Butlers of the Human world are actually pale imitations of the dedicated and happy Hob. You're fortunate. I don't cook, but apparently Floyd knows his way around a kitchen. Shall we? Before dinner grows cold?"

Jack and Rob didn't need to be told twice and headed to wash their hands.

"Wait. Where's Nickerson?" Eleanor asked. The trainer usually ate dinner with the family.

"I warned Nickerson I don't cook, and he wisely decided to use this time to explore the local eateries. Go on ahead, Eleanor. Take Flora in. I'd like a quick word with Camedon. Don't wait for me."

Eleanor would have liked to stay and hear what was said, but she and Flora headed in.

Chapter Twenty

FLOYD STOOD AT THE DINING ROOM DOOR, STARING STRAIGHT ahead. "Miss," he acknowledged them as they passed without looking at them.

Flora giggled, and Eleanor grinned. "We don't usually dine formally, Floyd. Dinner is family-style."

"Be that as it may, Miss, we are this evening. If you'd be seated?" the Hob suggested, still not making eye contact. He strode to the table and pulled out a chair.

Flora took it, and he moved to another chair, pulling it out for Eleanor. She sat and allowed the Hob to push in her chair. He took her napkin, opened it with a sharp snap, and set it on her lap. He then did the same for Flora.

He pulled his watch from his vest pocket and placed a monocle to his eye before checking the time. "I shall inquire on dinner. Slouching, Master Jack." He gave a dignified nod to the table and left the dining room.

They held their laughter in until they heard the creak of the swinging kitchen door.

"This rocks," Jack said.

"Sloucher," Flora said, straightening Bumper up in the seat beside her.

"Mum will *never* tolerate this," Eleanor said, laughing.

"Well, Mum isn't here, is she?" Jack said.

"I suspect she'll tolerate slouching awareness," Rob said.

"Jack's right. Mum's not home yet, and I'm going to enjoy this until she is."

The kitchen door creaked, and they sat straighter in their chairs. Floyd entered, this time in a chef's coat and hat, and houndstooth checked pants. He balanced a platter and loaves of fresh bread.

"This evening, a pappardelle with roasted root vegetable Bolognese, and multi-grain bolle," the Hob informed them in an affected Italian accent, presenting the food with a dramatic flourish. "With the bolle, diced local heirloom tomatoes, garlic, olive oil, fresh basil, and imported feta cheese. You will like, no?"

"What's the papa stuff?" asked Jack.

Floyd looked pained. "It is a pasta?" he told Jack, ending his words in a question, as if Jack were painfully simple. "A broad flat … how you say … ?" Floyd pretended to search for the right word in English. "Hearty! It is a hearty pasta! It is good, you eat!" He bustled around the table, serving everyone, and waited with an expectant smile until they tried it.

"This is excellent!" Rob said.

"Ahhh, *delizioso! Molto bene!* Eat!" Floyd directed, and sashayed back to the kitchen.

"I don't care if he has multiple personalities or an identity crisis. This rocks!"

"Is dinner ready?" Charlotte entered the dining room, Agnes behind her. The crow settled on the mantle.

"Yes!" Flora said. "And it's good!"

The librarian helped herself to pasta.

"Camedon feels, and I agree, that until this situation with the Noctivagi is resolved, the Elven Guard stays and accompanies you every time you leave the property." Charlotte's gaze settled on Jack.

"Don't look at me. I won't argue," he assured her. He shook his head, swallowing what was in his mouth. "I don't want to bump into Mr. Tall, Dark, and Crawling with Maggots alone."

"Excellent," she said. "This *is* delicious. I suspect your parents will adjust to having a Hob in the house. My mother did." She smiled, remembering. "Our Hob's name was Matthias. He was elderly and grouchy. I think his arthritis bothered him. I find myself sympathetic to that now."

"Why didn't you live here after your parents passed away?" Rob asked.

"My husband was uncomfortable with the Realm. Camedon offered to awaken his senses, but he was happier in the Human world. George was a wonderful man, but he was as practical as a doorknob, and he found the Realm too eventful. He worried about my safety. This house was too big for two people to rattle around in anyway."

"But it sat empty. Wouldn't it have been better to live in it?"

"Oh, it was never really empty," the librarian said. "It only appeared empty."

"Who lived here?"

"The question might be more accurately phrased, who *lives* here. You don't know?"

At the puzzled frowns her smile grew. "Far be it from me to ruin the surprise."

"You mean the Brownies?" Rob asked.

"The Brownies are not the only inhabitants at Black Ledge, but that's for you to discover on your own," she said.

"And Mum won't let us have a dog!" Jack snorted.

"Who needs a dog when we have everything else?" Flora pointed out.

"I want a dog," Jack said.

"So do I," Rob said.

"Dogs!" Agnes snorted. "Dogs are common."

"You felt that way about children, too," Jack reminded her.

The crow's beady, black eyes narrowed. "I still do."

Floyd entered, bearing a tray of pastry, and announced, "This evening, we have cannoli for dessert."

"What are cannoli?" asked Jack.

"I can see we have our work cut out for us." Floyd tsked and shook his head. "*Cannoli* are Sicilian pastry. Tubes of fried pasta, filled with sweet ricotta cheese. One never fills the cannoli until one is ready to serve the cannoli, else it's soggy and unpalatable." The Hob shuddered in revulsion. "I have chocolate and pistachio. For Miss Charlotte, I have a candied citron accompanied by a limoncello. And don't bother to ask what limoncello is as you can't have any, anyway."

Flora was quick. "Chocolate, please, Floyd."

Eleanor appreciated the distraction Floyd's entertaining personas provided. Flora showed no effects from the afternoon, but Eleanor suspected she'd sleep with her tonight. That was fine—Eleanor never minded Flora sleeping with her— but tomorrow Flora was getting the same instruction in defense the rest of them were getting.

"I'll try the pistachio," Rob said. "Unless you have a chocolate pistachio one?" he asked hopefully.

"Why yes, I do. I do have chocolate pistachio. Very good, Master Robert." Floyd bestowed a smile of such approval, it was almost embarrassing.

"What did Camedon say to you on the terrace?" Eleanor asked Mrs. Bradford.

"He told me what happened on the island. I never would have guessed Nob was Newlin. All these years ..." the librarian's voice faded, amazed by the prince's deception to remain close to his beloved.

"I hope they find Radek. I hope he isn't smart enough to drink from The Chalice."

"What did the Chalice look like?" Charlotte asked.

"Hard to say," Rob said. "It was covered in blood."

A door slammed and everyone jumped.

Chapter Twenty-One

GUNNR ENTERED THE DINING ROOM, TWO ELVEN GUARDS behind him. A man and a woman. Eleanor didn't recognize them, but they wore swords on their hips and moved with the same wary alertness as the others.

"Charlotte," he greeted the librarian.

Eleanor already knew by his expression, but she asked anyway. "Did you find him?"

He shook his head. "No. We followed the blood trail far into the state park, and then we lost it." He indicated the Elves behind him. "This is Tahlemar and Clayr. They are staying here tonight."

"I'm sure we'll all sleep better. Thank you," Charlotte said.

"The Pyskes have offered to help," he added.

Charlotte smiled. The two Elves did not.

"So now what?" asked Jack.

"We'll continue to hunt for his resting place and retrieve the Chalice. We have tonight and tomorrow before he'll be on the move. Camedon doesn't think Radek will dare drink from the Chalice—it may not occur to him, but even if it does, he probably won't."

"Why?" Rob asked.

"He wouldn't know which side to drink from."

"What do you mean?"

"The Chalice has two identical ends. The base and the bowl are shaped identically, much like an X. Only one end, though, has restorative properties—the other does not. Each end is equal, but opposes the other. Upright, it is called the Alabaster Chalice. Inverted, it is the Poisoned Chalice."

"But how would you know which side is okay and which isn't?"

"A symbol stamped into each cup's bottom reveals its properties. The Undine know, but the mystery surrounding it is a deterrent. Radek will be cautious with the Olde Magyk." Gunnr sounded confident, but he looked tired. Weary. He looked how Eleanor felt.

"So you're all set here," he told Charlotte. "They'll have the whole point covered. You needn't worry." They moved to the door.

"Thank you," the librarian said.

They left.

"Come on, Flora," Eleanor said. "Let's clear the table so we can get ready for bed."

"Can I sleep with you?" Flora asked. "And Bumper, too?"

"Yep."

"You guys want to watch a movie or something?" asked Jack.

"I'm too tired," Eleanor said. She wasn't, but she'd lie down with Flora until she was asleep.

"You guys go ahead. Jack and I'll clear the table," Rob offered.

Surprisingly, Jack did not argue. Eleanor and Flora headed upstairs.

She started a bath for Flora and left her to it. She could use the shower in her parents' bathroom. She was gathering pajamas when Flora walked in. "Whatcha doin'?" she asked, frowning.

"I'm going to take a shower in Mum and Dad's room while you have a tub."

"Can you wait until I'm done? Wait *here*?" Flora asked.

Eleanor hugged her. "Sure."

Eleanor sighed and sat at her desk, tidying it mindlessly. Someone, probably Jack, was watching TV downstairs, but the house was quiet. She picked up her sketchpad and a piece of charcoal, and doodled, but her mind was on the night.

She sent herself searching. She found Gunnr and tucked herself into a corner of his mind. She knew he was aware of her presence. He didn't acknowledge her, but he didn't close his mind to her.

He and the other warriors spread in formation and searched a mountain slope. Each craggy rock face and chasm, each ridge and depression. Evil touched the air, but it the source was indeterminable. A foul whiff, but nothing strong enough to follow.

Eleanor felt his satisfaction that they were close, though. Felt his determination and ruthlessness. They would find the monster.

Baelhar drew his attention to a crevice, and Gunnr dropped to his side. Something unnatural and dark tainted the night. Baelhar waved his hand, revealing woven protections. These were not delicate silver protections, intricately designed and woven, like those Eleanor had seen in Darnell. They were thick, coarse, and crude.

Gunnr and Baelhar studied the pattern, and Baelhar attempted to unravel them. As soon as his hands moved, black insects boiled from the crevice and attacked. Gunnr reduced them to ash with a wave of his hand.

Baelhar paused in his efforts.

"Keep going," Gunnr said. "I can deal with his defenses."

Baelhar began anew, concentrating on one side of the protections with careful hand movements, slow and methodical. At first it didn't appear to be working, but finally he extracted a single thread from the weave. It writhed, fighting his efforts. The ground shook and rocks rained down. Radek, lying deep in the mountain, was infuriated by their efforts, and his howl of outrage echoed in the night. Trees and debris fell around them, and Gunnr threw a protective shield over their heads to deflect the missiles Radek sent to thwart their efforts. Undeterred by the chaos surrounding him, Baelhar continued to tear apart the fibers protecting the cave's entrance.

Lightning flashed and wind howled. Radek may have been forced to earth to recover from his injuries, but he was far from powerless. He called on the worst Nature had to offer, but it wasn't enough to deter Gunnr and Baelhar.

The last of the protections fell away, and the crevice ripped open to reveal a narrow tunnel. Gunnr picked up a rock and threw it. Roots, magically fashioned into stiff skewers, sprang from the walls. Had they stepped into the tunnel, the roots would have impaled them.

"That wouldn't have felt good," Baelhar noted dryly.

"Dissolve to mist. He'll have rigged the entire chamber," Gunnr said.

Maethoron and Handrven appeared behind them.

"Wait here in case he gets past us," Baelhar told them.

Gunnr smiled. "He's not getting past us." Gunnr gathered a bolt of energy in his hands and sent an explosion into the tunnel. The flash singed everything contained therein.

Radek bellowed his fury.

Gunnr laughed, satisfied he'd scored a blow.

"Still a people person, I see," Baelhar said.

Baelhar and Gunnr's forms blurred and disappeared.

Tucked in his mind, Eleanor wondered at the weightlessness she experienced through their connection. Gravity and physical limitations fell away and his spirit soared, unrestrained. Even in a dangerous situation, it was electrifying.

They moved through to the tunnel's end, regained their corporeal forms and examined the space for a disturbance. Magic always left a trace, even if the trace was the void concealing it.

The tunnel was hot, and noxious fumes stung their eyes. Gunnr pointed at the ceiling. Every other surface showed disturbances in the rock formation, but the ceiling was unblemished. Noticeably so. Gunnr motioned Baelhar to the side of the tunnel, and blasted the ceiling with energy. Ugly protections flashed, momentarily visible, but nothing else happened. Gunnr reached out and grabbed them, ripping them down. The strands struggled and fought, and Eleanor felt them burning his hand, but he held on until they gave, falling to the floor in a slithering pile of nastiness. Baelhar incinerated them.

A hole in the ceiling yawned, and dirt fell from the edges. Something above moved, disturbing the soil. Gunnr waved his hand, and larger clumps of dirt fell, revealing a bloodstained track that disappeared farther into the soil. Radek was on the run, burrowing through the soil.

Gunnr charged into the hole after him. Eleanor fought a feeling of claustrophobia, but she held the connection as he pursued the Noctivagi through the narrow track. Through Gunnr's eyes, she saw the distance between them closing. Just as he reached to grab Radek's ankle, they burst forth into the night through a crack in the mountain's surface.

Radek dissolved in the night air, droplets of fresh blood the only evidence of his presence, and they spread, the stain on the night sky fading away.

Frustrated, Gunnr landed on the rock face. Baelhar appeared next to him, and then Handrven and Maethoron.

"He didn't have the Chalice!" Baelhar said.

"No. He's hidden it away from his resting place. Recklessness isn't what's kept him alive all these years. The chimney he'd left for escape was brilliantly concealed," Gunnr said.

Taunting laughter floated on the wind, and in the recesses of Gunnr's mind, Eleanor's skin crawled.

"Your turn, El." Flora's voice ripped Eleanor from Gunnr's mind.

Chapter Twenty-Two

"EL?" FLORA PROMPTED.

"Right here, Florie," Eleanor said.

"I'm done in the bathroom."

"Why don't you go watch TV with Jack while I take my shower?"

"'Kay. Yell when you're out." Flora went into her room, likely to grab Bumper, and then her footsteps thumped down the stairs.

Eleanor took her pajamas to their bathroom, set them on the counter, and then started the shower. She turned back to get a clean a towel and washcloth, and saw one of each on the counter next to her pajamas. They hadn't been there a minute ago. Eleanor stood, looking at them. They definitely had *not* been there a moment before.

"Alright. Who's in here?"

A blond head popped up behind the tub. At first Eleanor thought it was Martin, but then was relieved to see it was a woman.

"Who are you?"

"Martha," she whispered. She smiled, and it lit up her small face.

"Why are you whispering?"

"Brighty says we aren't to bother you," the brownie said.

"Have you been the one making my bed and picking up

my bedroom?"

Martha beamed, and nodded.

"Thank you."

"Happy trails." The diminutive woman smiled and disappeared.

Eleanor knew she was gone, but she peeked behind the tub before she finished undressing and got in the shower. The hot water felt wonderful, and desperate to remove the salt and grime, Eleanor scrubbed her skin until it stung. Finally, she felt as clean inside as she was outside. She leaned against the tile to let the hot water loosen the knotted, sore muscles in her back.

She was still standing there when the lights went out, leaving her in darkness.

She shut off the water and felt for her towel, drying off quickly and wrapping the towel around her head. She pulled her pajamas on, felt around the vanity for her hairbrush, and stuck her head outside the door. "Hey?" she called.

"Eleanor?" Jack answered.

"Yeah, what's going on?"

"Hang on, I have a flashlight," Jack said from the stairs. He shined the flashlight so she could see.

"Come here first. I need something on my feet and I can't see."

Jack came the rest of way. "Heaven forbid your feet be soiled touching the same floor we peasants use."

"Shut up, Jack." Eleanor took his flashlight and returned to her room. She grabbed her moccasins and rejoined him in the hall.

"Better?"

"Yeah. Thanks."

They went back downstairs.

"We're in the library," he said, heading down the hall.

Through the glass doors, lights twinkled on the waterfront across the harbor. The electricity wasn't out in town.

Charlotte was lighting more candles and speaking to one of the Elven Guards. When Eleanor pointed to the lights across the harbor Charlotte nodded, concern evident on her face. She'd seen it.

"Tahlemar is checking the extent of the power failure," the guard Clayr told her.

"Is there power in the barn?"

"There isn't any power on the point at all." The Elf's tone was cautious.

"What about Nickerson? Has anyone checked on him?"

"I don't believe he's back," Charlotte assured her.

Eleanor sat next to Flora and pulled a throw over them. She reached for Gunnr.

"Our power's out."

"When?"

"A few minutes ago."

"Is Camedon still there?"

"No, just us, Charlotte, and guards. One is talking to Charlotte—the woman."

"Clayr."

"She said Tahlemar was checking if anything beyond the point was out. There are lights across the harbor."

"We'll be right there."

"We're fine. The point is protected, and Charlotte is here. Someone probably hit a pole, or all of Radek's lightning struck one."

"Probably. Better to be cautious, though. We're not far."

"Where is Camedon?

"I have no idea."

"Is he—"

Gunnr cut her off, his tone hard. *"Lock the doors, stay together, and wait for us to come to you. Don't go outside."*

"Why? What's going on?"

"There's power at the street. The power to the point is underground—if you don't have power, someone's shut it off at the house. Baelhar cannot rouse Tahlemar on our common path."

Dread hit Eleanor's stomach like a stone.

"But the point is protected!"

"From Noctivagi, but not those under their control. Lock the doors and don't let anyone in until you see us."

Eleanor stood and casually made her way to Charlotte and the guard, Clayr. So as not to frighten Flora, she said softly, "We need to lock the doors. Gunnr and the others are on their way."

Charlotte and Clayr were quick to respond. Clayr moved to the hall door, and Charlotte to the doors on the terrace.

"I feel a draft. Did you shut these doors tightly, Jack?" the librarian asked, making her way to them as if she were checking. The lock clicked, and then Charlotte moved to the others.

Eleanor shivered. Gunnr was right—something was out there. The taint of evil approached the house. Sly and insidious, it was out there.

Something rattled the door, startling Charlotte. She lurched back and Clayr leapt, drawing her sword.

"It's us," Baelhar called.

Clayr opened the door.

Gunnr and Baelhar entered. "Maethoron and Handrven are searching the point."

"No sign of Tahlemar?" Clayr asked.

"No, not yet. We'll find him, though. In the meantime, we'll wait here." Gunnr had no more gotten the words out when something slammed against the door they'd entered moments before.

The glass shattered and something crashed into the room, taking the door right off the hinges.

Baelhar rushed it, Clayr and Gunnr on his heels.

Charlotte and Eleanor both moved to Flora, but Jack reached her first and pulled her to the floor, keeping the sofa between them and the fighting.

Baelhar tackled the figure. They rolled out the door and across the terrace.

Eleanor moved to the window, but she still couldn't see, so she buried herself in Gunnr's mind.

Baelhar restrained the figure face down. Pyskes buzzed, brandishing pieces of wire and toothpicks as swords. They surrounded it, hovering, and stabbing at it.

Felix flew to Gunnr and said, "Tahlemar is in the barn. It knocked him out and tied him with wire."

"It? What is it?" Baelhar asked.

Gunnr wrenched the figure up by the neck. "A Human. He must be under compulsion," Gunnr said. He lifted the intruder's face and Eleanor gasped.

"Stop!" she yelled. She ran onto the terrace and grabbed Gunnr's arm. "It's Nickerson! Stop!"

Gunnr's hold relaxed. "You sure?"

She nodded. "Is he hurt?" His eyes were glassy and unfocused. He swiped at Gunnr, but his efforts were weak.

Gunnr examined him and said, "No, he isn't hurt. He's only under Radek's compulsion."

"Can you remove it?"

"Yes. He'll probably have a headache from taking out the door, but we can remove the compulsion. He won't remember a thing." He stared into Nickerson's eyes and, layering his voice thick with hypnotic suggestion, said, *"When you wake you will be free from all influences on your mind, except this: you will remember nothing of this incident. Your last memory will be coming home and going to bed. You will sleep, undisturbed, all night."* He then added, *"And tomorrow, you will have renewed health, energy, and vitality."*

The old man's eyes closed, and his body relaxed. Gunnr carried him back into the library and laid him gently on the couch.

"That's creepy."

"But effective."

Charlotte hovered and tucked the throw around him. "You're certain he'll be all right?"

"He'll be fine." Gunnr looked at the door and waved his hand. The door righted itself, reattached to the jamb, and the glass reassembled in the panes as if it were a movie played in reverse.

"Where were *you* when I threw my baseball through the living room window?" Jack said.

Gunnr smiled, but he'd already moved on to the next course of action. "Maethoron and Handrven will take Nickerson to the carriage house, leave him in his bed, and then find Tahlemar. Baelhar and I will continue to search for Radek. The rest of you will stay here." He gave Eleanor her negative answer before she could even ask. "Clayr, I'd like you to stay in the house. The others can keep a watch outside."

"We'll help!" Felix offered, holding his sword high.

"Good. The more, the better. You have an edge we don't. You're familiar with the property, and you notice things others overlook." He instructed Clayr, "After everyone leaves, place protections on the doors and windows."

"All right."

Maethoron lifted the sleeping Nickerson as if he was a small boy, and Handrven opened the door for him. They left, Pyskes trailing after them, tiny swords at the ready.

"We'll be fine, Gunnr," Charlotte assured him.

"You're certain?"

"Yes. Quite certain. We'll be fine. I've been through this a time or two."

He smiled, but it was a sad smile. "I know."

Charlotte patted him on the shoulder and herded him and Baelhar to the door. "Off with you. Be careful." She closed the door behind them. "We must all try to get some sleep."

Clayr spoke. "I'm going to ward the house with protections. I'll start in the bedrooms so I won't keep you up."

"Do whatever you need to do, dear. It won't bother us at all. I appreciate you staying tonight."

The Elf smiled, and Eleanor realized how young she was. She didn't have the wariness the other Warriors did. "It's a nice change. I'm still in training to be a Warrior of the Realm, and I usually get the rainy night shifts. Or worse, the snowy ones. The others can grumble, but I'll take Driscoll Duty any day."

"Is that what they call it? *Driscoll Duty?*" asked Jack, incredulous and insulted.

Clayr cringed when she realized what she'd said. "Oh, that isn't what I meant. Most of the Elven Guard want assignments with some action. Risk. The point has protections placed on it, so they don't feel useful when they are here."

"They want action? I'll give them some action," Jack muttered.

Chapter Twenty-Three

It felt as if Eleanor had just closed her eyes when a voice wrenched them open.

"*You must go to him.*"

She was dreaming. She closed her eyes.

"*Wake and prepare!*" the raspy voice commanded.

It couldn't be. "*Motte?*"

"*Yes!*"

"*Why are you in my head?*"

"*There is no time to explain. You must move, child. This moment decides time!*"

Eleanor scrambled from her bed, not understanding, but recognizing the urgency in the Gargoyle's voice.

She fumbled in the darkness for clothes. Her bureau drawer was stuck. When she worked it, something fell to the floor.

"Eleanor? Are you all right?" Clayr inquired from the hall.

"Ah, yeah. Fine."

"*She will take you to him,*" Motte instructed.

"What?" Eleanor asked.

"I asked if you needed help," Clayr said.

"Sorry, not you," Eleanor said.

"What?" Clayr asked, alarmed, and entered the room holding a ball of soft light aloft. "Why are you getting dressed?"

"*She must take you to him. The others won't. Gunnr must not know you are coming. You must hurry!*" The Gargoyle was

— 168 —

becoming agitated.

"Sorry, I … ah … I need you to take me somewhere. I can't really explain. Well … I can, but you'll think I'm crazy. I need you to trust me. Don't ask the other guards because they won't let us go, but we have to. Now." She tied her hikers and grabbed the knives Gunnr had given her.

"We can't leave, Eleanor. It isn't safe—"

"No, we have to. Motte says I have to. Right now. She's dreadful, but she wouldn't lie. Not about Gunnr. Not about something like this. Please. We must listen to her."

"I don't understand. Who is Motte?"

"Motte is Gunnr's Gargoyle."

"I do not belong to Gunnr."

"Give me a minute!" Eleanor snapped.

Clayr looked astonished. "His Gargoyle?"

"Yes! And she knows things. Probably awful things, but she's loyal to Gunnr and if she's calling to me, it's important. Please, Clayr. We must go. Now."

Eleanor headed downstairs and stopped for a coat. Clayr followed, confused and worried.

"I don't know what to do. I can't leave Charlotte and your brothers and sister unprotected …" Clayr's voice trailed off.

Eleanor held her finger to her lips, and went to the door. "As soon as we're away from the point, you can tell Maethoron or one of the other guards," she whispered.

Clayr studied her for a moment, and then raised her hands and removed the safeguards from the door.

"And where might you be sneaking off to, Miss?"

Eleanor groaned. It was Floyd, in a nightshirt and cap.

"Clayr is taking me to check on Nickerson. I'm worried and I can't sleep. We'll be back in a few minutes. Everything is fine."

"Very good, Miss," Floyd said.

"Sorry to disturb you."

"I'll just wait here and make sure you are okay," the Hob said.

Eleanor kept her tone light. "If we'll be more than a few minutes, we'll send Maethoron to guard the house."

"Very good, Miss."

"You must hurry!"

"I know!" Eleanor said.

"Pardon?" Floyd frowned.

"Sorry, not you."

Floyd's frown grew.

Clayr saved Eleanor from any more awkwardness. "Lock the door behind us, Floyd." They stepped onto the terrace.

Clayr asked, "Where are we going?"

"I don't know."

"They're at the river," Motte said, answering her question before she could even ask.

"What part?"

"Where it is wide and swift.

Eleanor's patience was gone. *"Can you be a little less cryptic?"*

"Where the Undine held the celebration," Motte said.

"Where the Undine held the celebration," Eleanor told the Elf.

"Climb on my back, and wrap your arms around my neck," Clayr said. She dropped one knee to the ground, and wrapped her arms around Eleanor's legs, clasping her tightly. "All set?"

"Yes."

"Hold on." Clayr launched herself into the air.

The bright moon glinted off the harbor and slate rooftops, and illuminated fields and open areas.

"Stay low," Eleanor said.

Clayr chuckled and asked, "Don't like heights?"

"No, I don't want the other guards to see us."

"I only told Tahlemar what we are doing," Clayr said, but she did stay low, skimming the treetops. "He is going to tell Maethoron in a few moments, and one of them will follow us."

"He won't stop us?" Eleanor asked.

"No. But I had to tell one of them," Clayr said. "Tahlemar was the best choice."

They passed the end of the point, and Eleanor felt the evil in the air. She shivered.

"Hurry," she urged Clayr.

"You must close your mind to him. He'll sense your presence," Motte said.

"I don't know how."

"You do, and you must," the Gargoyle insisted.

"I'll lose contact with you, too."

"You can now. You won't need me. Close your mind!"

"How will I know what to do?"

"You'll know."

Motte's words did not assure Eleanor. She'd never felt so confused or uncertain. Motte was nasty, but she wouldn't lie. What was about to happen was important, even though she didn't know why, or how.

As they approached the state park, anxiety built. They needed to hurry, but she didn't know how to keep Gunnr unaware of her presence. She'd been trying to open connections, not build walls, and Motte's words made her want to reach for him, not block him.

She had to trust Motte. And herself. She took a deep breath, calmed herself, and concentrated. Visualized. She started with a wall, much like Gunnr's protective shields, dark, like the night, undetectable and indiscernible. It surrounded her mind, silencing her thoughts and feelings to anything beyond it. She hoped.

"She wants me to cloak my presence," Eleanor said.

"I can do that," Clayr said.

"She meant my mind," Eleanor explained.

"My protection will reinforce yours," Clayr said.

Clayr's assurances eased Eleanor's mind slightly. They flew onward, approaching the entrance to the old logging road. Clayr dropped beneath the overhanging limbs and flew along the road, drawing closer and closer to the place Motte had named. The forest was darker, and Eleanor was glad she knew this road so well. She had to trust Motte. And herself. She repeated that in her mind.

"Land here," Eleanor said as they passed over the spot where Gunnr had switched her clothes.

Clayr landed gently, and Eleanor slid off her back.

The evil hung thick and oily in the air, not threatening her, just present. Too hard to determine the direction to head. "I don't know. Listen—"

Lightning forked the sky, striking and shaking the ground somewhere ahead of them.

Eleanor took off, heedless of the danger. Clayr followed, alert and on guard.

Eleanor ran down the road, but slowed and slipped into the woods as she neared the clearing. She sidled through the trees to a large rock on the edge of the clearing. Heeding Motte's warning, she kept her mind blank as she peeked around the boulder.

Radek obviously hadn't had a problem replacing the Noctivagi who'd perished, as another stood at his side facing Gunnr and Baelhar.

Clayr stood, ready to join the fight, but Eleanor quickly

grabbed her arm and pulled her back down. Clayr's presence would give them away. Remembering Nob, Eleanor didn't want to distract Gunnr or Baelhar.

The Noctivagus circled Baelhar, looking for vulnerability, a weakness. He raised his hands, summoned a jagged branch from a nearby spruce tree, and fired it at Baelhar as if it were a missile. Baelhar stepped aside, and reached out and caught the projectile neatly. He returned it in one fluid movement, impaling the Noctivagus's leg. The Noctivagus roared and yanked the branch out. Dark, foul blood gushed down his rotting leg, hitting the ground in a steaming hiss. The Noctivagus attacked, a bellowing blur of claws and fangs, tackled Baelhar, and the two rolled across the ground.

Baelhar's sword lay where it dropped, and Radek held his hand out, calling the discarded weapon to him. He laughed, triumphant, and waved it at Gunnr.

Gunnr tipped his head and acknowledged Radek's acquisition with a wry smile. "You'll need that."

"You waste yourself, Gunnr. Set your sword down. Join us." Radek jerked his head toward the woods to where the Chalice lay on the ground. "We have one of the Restoratives—we'll get the others and complete the ritual correctly this time. We will have what we sought."

Gunnr snorted. "Did you learn nothing about the dangers of the Olde Magyk the first time?"

"You always were a fool," Radek said. He lunged and slashed at Gunnr.

Gunnr deflected the blow, and they met, inches apart, swords locked against each other. Each struggled to overpower the other, but their strengths were matched. Radek jumped back and shoved, swinging at Gunnr's head. Gunnr ducked, and bringing his sword up, stuck it in Radek's side, but his swing was late and weakened the blow. The Noctivagus snarled and fell back.

Gunnr pursued, not allowing him a moment's reprieve, and thrust his sword again. Radek's form shifted, transforming to a rat and dropping to the ground. He ran between Gunnr's feet, and Gunnr stepped on his tail, preventing his escape. Radek shifted back to the Noctivagus form and rolled for his sword, but Gunnr grabbed him around the neck and wrenched.

The evil that flashed across Radek's face was the only warning. His shape blurred and he shifted again.

Radek had assumed Eleanor's own shape.

When Gunnr saw his hands around the neck of an illusion of Eleanor, he recoiled and let go.

Radek thrust his sword through Gunnr's heart.

Eleanor screamed and leapt from behind the tree.

Gunnr seemed frozen, struggling between defending himself and striking a killing blow at what he knew was Eleanor's illusion.

He fell backward, Radek and his sword staying with him all the way to the ground.

Radek resumed his own shape, and with an evil smile, twisted the sword in Gunnr's chest back and forth. Radek reached down, wiped the bright blood that flowed heavily from Gunnr's wound, and licked his fingers.

Eleanor pulled two knives from the sheath on her belt and threw them in rapid succession at the Noctivagus, but she threw wildly and only one hit, sinking deeply into his neck. She ran toward them, Clayr following.

Radek's smile grew when he saw his attacker. "Ahhh. The consolation prize." He leaned down and told Gunnr, "I'll be taking her, too." Radek reached to pull Eleanor's knife from his neck.

With a final burst of strength, Gunnr sat up. He swung his sword in a disemboweling slice across Radek's mid-section. The Noctivagus stilled, frozen by the severity of the blow. Blood and intestines spilled from the wound.

Radek grasped his stomach, holding himself together. His body blurred to a silhouette, and then disappeared. A haze of dark bloody mist moved through the air, and slowly faded from view.

Gunnr collapsed.

Eleanor reached his side and sunk to her knees beside him. He squeezed her hand.

"*You told me to take off his head. I tried,*" he said.

Eleanor brushed his hair from his face. "*Hang on.*"

Baelhar was almost to them. He pulled energy from the skies as he ran to their sides, and when he dropped to his knees, he placed both hands on Gunnr's chest. White light entered the gaping wound, but Baelhar looked to Eleanor, frustrated and desperate.

"What?" Eleanor whispered, petrified.

"I can't *heil* this—his heart is in shreds. He'll bleed out before I can repair the damage. He needs blood."

"I'll give him blood." She extended her forearm toward the sword's blade.

Baelhar shook his head. "There isn't time." He told Gunnr apologetically, "I have to pull this out."

"Do me a favor. Do it … after." Gunnr's voice faded.

"Don't be ridiculous. Hold on," Baelhar told him, but his tight expression belied his reassuring voice.

"Take her to Sol, Baelhar. Matters. She's … Sol'll … Motte …"

Eleanor grabbed his hand, desperately holding on. She felt him sliding from them, and her insides turned to ice. She looked to Baelhar, "Do something!"

"*Azathela! We need the healer!*" Baelhar's voice thundered in Eleanor's head. Aloud, he said, "Get the Chalice, Clayr, and fill it with water. Eleanor, hold your connection with him. With everything you have. Don't let him slide away."

Eleanor pushed past Gunnr's defenses, placing herself wholly in his mind, and held his spirit to her. He offered little resistance in his weakened state. His suffering was unbearable, and she breathed deeply, taking as of the pain into her as she could.

"*Don't,*" he said.

"*Stop reading my mind,*" she said, giving him the answer he expected, but inside she was choking.

He saw through it, all the same. "*Let go, Eleanor. Before I pass.*" His voice thready, but earnest.

She didn't answer, not wanting him to waste energy arguing, but reinforced their connection, holding it in the light in her mind.

"Hurry, Clayr!" Baelhar yelled.

"I don't know which side to fill," Clayr told him, frantic.

"Just fill it!" Baelhar urged, but Eleanor realized the problem and she felt hope slipping away.

The Chalice was dual-ended and Clayr could only fill one side. They didn't have time to figure which one was the correct one.

Baelhar added, "I'll drink from it first."

Stunned Baelhar would endanger his life, Eleanor racked her brain, trying to remember what Gunnr had told them about the Chalice. Something about a symbol stamped into the bottom only the Undine could read. If only she could touch it—

"Clayr! Bring it to me!" Eleanor yelled. At the Elf's hesitation, she urged, "Hurry!"

Clayr ran to Eleanor's side and handed her the Chalice. Eleanor had to release Gunnr's hand to take it. She examined the Chalice quickly and chose an end. She reached in and ran her finger over the raised symbol at the bottom. Eleanor felt a familiar thrum of energy and breathed a sigh of relief.

She pulled her hand from the cup and looked at the symbol, understanding. Quickly, she tipped the Chalice and did the same thing with the other end, confirming what she saw.

Eleanor handed the Chalice to Clayr, right side up. "This end. Fill it."

Clayr reached toward the river, conjuring a silver stream of water to the chalice.

Eleanor took Gunnr's hand again. It was cool. His heartbeat had become an infrequent spasm, and his spirit was pulling away. Eleanor went with it, holding on with everything she had. Physically, mentally, and emotionally.

"*Let go.*"

"*You will not leave,*" she said, willing it so. She felt Motte merge her own strength and determination. The Gargoyle held Gunnr's spirit to them with the same ferocity Eleanor did. A strange tingling wrapped them in a flowing and ageless energy. Eleanor knew the energy came from Motte, though she didn't know what it was. She didn't care. She embraced it. Dark and old, it bound the three of them together tightly in a cloak of comfort.

"Eleanor!" Clayr said, pulling Eleanor back from the web of Motte's magic. She out held the Chalice, water dripping.

"Make him drink," Eleanor told them.

Baelhar knelt and held it to Gunnr's lips. He hesitated for a moment, and looked at Eleanor. She nodded, urging him to hurry. Gunnr was far gone, and couldn't drink on his own. Baelhar gently opened his mouth and poured the water in. Clayr massaged Gunnr's throat, forcing him to swallow.

Gunnr choked and coughed. Connected so completely, Eleanor felt the blade work deeper with every cough. She ground her teeth, almost unable to bear the staggering pain, but gasped, "More."

Baelhar continued to pour the liquid down Gunnr's throat. Finally, it was gone, but nothing happened.

Several Elves materialized beside them. Baelhar stood, and Azathela, the Elven *Heiler*, took his place at Gunnr's side. Queen Solvanha knelt beside her and took Gunnr's other hand.

Azathela placed her hands on Gunnr's chest, cupping the wound around the sword. "I can't *heil* this from the outside—I must repair the damage from the inside if he is to recover. When I enter his body you must pull the sword straight out. Don't turn it or angle it. It must slide out exactly as it is. Can you do this?"

Baelhar nodded.

"Eleanor, continue holding his spirit to you. Don't allow him to move away. Solvanha, merge your energy with Eleanor." Azathela didn't wait for them to agree, but focused her being into an orb of *heiling* energy and entered the wound. The Elven *Heiler's* body appeared an empty shell. In another circumstance, Eleanor would have been fascinated by what she was witnessing, but Gunnr's energy was fading in her mind,

Why hadn't the Chalice worked? Had the damage to his heart been too great, or had they taken too long?

Baelhar placed both of his hands on the sword, and steeling himself, slid it out in one swift movement. The moment the tip of the sword cleared the wound, electricity arced, and Gunnr's body spasmed violently.

Azathela was snapped back into her own body, and everyone close to Gunnr was thrown several feet.

Gunnr arched off the ground, twisting and writhing. Frowns

and uncertainty crossed the others' faces, but relief flooded Eleanor. Baelhar laughed outright.

They'd seen this happen already today. To Newlin.

Gunnr's body twisted and writhed, groaned and gasped. His eyes opened, staring blankly, and closed.

Eleanor crawled back to him and took his hand. She forced herself into his mind and saw chaos and pain, but she pushed reassurance and calm to him through the violent convulsions.

Energy crackled in flashes and arcs, and then stilled, leaving his body limp and motionless on the ground.

Eleanor clutched his hand and waited. Nothing happened for several moments, and then she felt a slight squeeze.

Chapter Twenty-Four

THE SKY LIGHTENED AT DAWN'S APPROACH. GUNNR RESTED, his back against a tree, and watched Baelhar and Clayr incinerate the remains of the Noctivagi and evidence of the battle. Eleanor sat next to him, her head on his shoulder, the Chalice in her lap. Her eyes were closed, but she was awake.

Queen Solvanha hovered, torn between helping Baelhar and Clayr, and checking Gunnr.

He tipped his head back and closed his eyes. "Sit, Sol. You're driving me crazy," he said.

Most of the Elves who'd arrived with the *Heiler* and Queen Solvanha had left, but a few lingered, and when Queen Solvanha finally sat they approached. One led, two others following.

Eleanor didn't pay much attention to their hesitancy until she saw the guarded look on the Elf's face when he glanced at Queen Solvanha. They were Night Elves, like Gunnr.

The Elf in the middle spoke for all three. "Gunnr."

Gunnr opened his eyes. "Lassar."

The two regarded each other, their expressions revealing nothing.

After a moment, Lassar shook his head. "Glad you're all right."

Gunnr shrugged, a wry expression on his face. "Fortune favors fools, and all that." He looked to other two Elves and greeted them. "Koravel. Ilus."

"We would have arrived sooner—had you asked for our assistance," one of the Night Elves said.

Gunnr gave him a half smile. "There wasn't time to send invitations to the party."

"Elders aren't Warriors of the Realm," the third Night Elf stated, and the other two nodded.

"I'm not an Elder," Gunnr reminded him.

"You're our Elder," Lassar argued with a quick, defiant look at Queen Solvanha.

Gunnr started to speak, but Queen Solvanha cut him off. "He's correct. You are the recognized Elder of the Night Elves, regardless of you being a Warrior of the Realm," she paused. "The most important word in that is Elves. You," including the others with a gesture, "were born Elves, and you've fought to remain Elves. It will take diplomacy, and maybe even some Magyk, but the exile imposed should be lifted on those who abide by the terms of the Accord. King Vitr will agree."

Baelhar caught Eleanor's eye and gave her a smug look. *"Told you I'd talk to Solvanha,"* he said on their private path.

Gunnr gave no indication he'd heard Baelhar. His attention was on his sister. Eleanor didn't need to feel the emotion from him to know Solvanha's words had impacted him. It showed on his face. The three Night Elves seemed wary, but they were receptive to the Elven Queen's words.

"Gunnr, Queen Solvanha," Lassar, said, inclining his head to each, as did the other two Elves.

The Night Elf's gaze moved to Eleanor. His face was expressionless, but there was something predatory and assessing in his eyes, and it creeped her out. She was stunned when he tipped his head and acknowledged her.

"Eleanor."

Their shapes blurred, and they disappeared.

She looked to Gunnr. "How does he know who I am?"

"How could he not know who you are? He'd have to live under a rock. Oh, wait …" Gunnr said, humor crinkling his eyes. "He knows who you are."

"How come I've never met any of them?"

"They keep to themselves. They were at the Solstice ceremony, but didn't linger."

"How many Night Elves are there?

"Originally there were nine. There are seven of us left." Gunnr turned to his sister. "The offer to rescind the exile? Decent of you, Sol. I don't know how much support you'll have, but the gesture was appreciated. *Is* appreciated."

Queen Solvanha said, "Vitr will agree."

"Well, in any case, you've gained six more appreciative supporters," Gunnr said.

Queen Solvanha's gaze fell on Eleanor. "Once again, I am indebted to you."

Eleanor dismissed the gratitude. "It was Motte."

"Gunnr's Gargoyle?"

"I don't belong to Gunnr."

"Yes. She woke me. Told me to come."

"Thank heavens you listened," said Solvanha. "One rarely understands Gargoyles. Their words are cryptic, but they know things. They understand the Songs of the Ley Lines."

At Eleanor's puzzled expression, Queen Solvanha explained.

"The Ley Lines are part of the Earth, and they carry the Earth's magic—the Olde Magyk. They are similar to rivers, but instead of water, their currents are Energy, Magyk, and Time. What has been, what is, and prophesies of what will be flow through the Ley Lines. The echoes of those are the Songs of the

Ley Lines. Gargoyles, being children of the Earth, are at home in the Ley Lines. They travel them, and they hear and understand the songs. Nothing is absolute, choices affect the course of events, but when a Gargoyle speaks, one should listen. They know things."

"I can't take any credit for that. I didn't know about Gargoyles, but she doesn't like me, so I knew if she reached out to me, it must be important." Uncomfortable with the praise, she confessed, "She still creeps me out."

"But you listened," Gunnr said. "For whatever reason, you listened, and I'm grateful." He gave her an amused look. "I suspect you'll see an improvement in Motte's attitude."

Eleanor doubted it, but kept her skepticism regarding the leathery beast to herself.

Baelhar and Clayr joined them.

"Get it all?" Gunnr asked.

"Yes."

"Thank yo—"

Baelhar cut him off. "You'd do the same. I'm more interested in how Eleanor knew which end of the Chalice to fill."

All attention returned to Eleanor. She lifted the Chalice and tipped it, showing them the inside of one end. Raised in relief at the bottom of the cup was a triangle. She tipped the Chalice to show them the symbol in the other end. The symbol consisted of three dots, spread in the shape of a triangle and enclosed in a circle. She received blank looks from all but Gunnr, who suddenly understood.

"I understand written languages when I touch them, even symbols," she explained. "When I touched this symbol I understood it to mean Aqua Vitae—water of life." She turned the Chalice and showed the inside of the other end. "This symbol stood for Caput Mortuum, or worthless remains. It wasn't brain surgery."

"Might as well have been. For us," Clayr said.

"Incoming." Baelhar pointed toward the logging road.

Camedon and Newlin approached, assessing the group and looking around at the trampled clearing.

"So glad you could join us," Baelhar said.

Camedon smiled. "You've been spending too much time with Jack."

"Yes, I have," Baelhar said.

Newlin's tense expression relaxed when he saw the Chalice sitting in Eleanor's lap. "You retrieved it."

Eleanor held it out to him. Newlin reached for it, but hesitated and looked to Camedon. The Keeper nodded.

Newlin tipped the Chalice to Gunnr, as if toasting him. "Not much fun, is it?"

"No, can't say I care to do it again anytime soon."

"And Radek?" Newlin asked.

"Escaped," Gunnr said.

"It won't be the last we hear of him," Camedon said.

"No," Gunnr agreed. "He's after the Artifacts. He said as much. Your concerns were justified, Camedon."

"It was only a matter of time before he made his move. They've been changing more Beings into Noctivagi than they've been killing. There's a reason. Is Radek the top of that food chain, or is he following the orders of another?"

"I don't know," Gunnr said. "He said *we*, but he was always one to give the orders, not follow them." He looked to Baelhar and Queen Solvanha. They both nodded. "He's grown even more powerful."

The Keeper considered Gunnr's words. "No matter. We'll

alert the Keepers, assemble that network. There are always signs, if one knows what to look for. We'll be able to figure out where he's been, what's he's been doing in recent years."

"The Artifacts of the Four Restoratives? I'll relinquish the Alabaster Chalice to ensure its safety," Newlin offered.

Camedon shrugged. "I don't think anyone can offer better protection than those who are doing so right now, but we'll address it. You and the others will be included in the discussion, Newlin. To Newlin and Queen Solvanha both, he said, "You could both come with me now."

Queen Solvanha stood. "We're done here. Gunnr? We'll speak later. Let me know when you rise?"

"Yes." He smiled. "Might be a few days."

"Very good," Camedon said. "You'll all excuse us?"

The three vanished.

Baelhar stood. "I'll take Eleanor back," he said.

"I can," Clayr offered.

"No. I will." Gunnr stood. "If you two would check on the guard at the point? See to everything there?" He held out a hand and helped Eleanor to her feet. "Ready, Killer?"

"I like that nickname."

Gunnr smiled. "*Of course you do.*" He lifted her, and they took the air. They'd flown about half the length of the logging road when Eleanor clenched his arm and pointed to the ground. Gunnr landed lightly and set her down. She bent over, retching. When she stood, he handed her a handkerchief he'd fashioned with magic.

"Is it me?" he asked.

"Apparently." Eleanor wiped her mouth. "I didn't get sick with Clayr."

His smile twitched at her prickliness, but he said, "It's probably a delayed reaction to the violence," he told her. "The physical stress of the situation. Brave as you are, it's upsetting, and one has to process it. I suspect being physically ill is symbolic of expelling it, or at least the lingering adrenaline in your system. It's a healthy reaction. Better?"

"Yeah." Eleanor dismissed his psychological mumbo jumbo, but she did feel better.

Gunnr started to pick her up and she stopped him. "Can I ride on your back? Face forward? It might help."

He bent so she could wrap her arms around his neck. When she was settled, they resumed their journey to Black Ledge. The wind in her face did make her feel better.

He landed by the birch trees beside the front drive, bent for her to slide off his back, then faced her. "What are we going to tell your parents this time?"

"That everything turned out fine, thanks to Clayr."

His eyebrow went up, and he eyed her, amused.

"Less is more," she added.

"I'm glad I'm not your parent. The rest of your teenage years should be a joy."

Eleanor scoffed. "Oh, please. Like I'll be able to get away with anything. I have parents, two brothers, an entire Elven Guard following me around, and people in my head."

"Is it too much?"

Eleanor thought about his question. "No, but it might be if I didn't have Rob, Jack, and Flora. If I was alone with this secret."

"What about friends?"

"My best friend is away for the summer—at her father's. Katy'll be back right before school starts, but she's the only one who might be a problem. She's practically part of the family."

"We'll figure it out," he said, reminding himself to ask

Charlotte about the girl. Every Human newly *aware* brought complications to be sorted out, but they did always seem to get sorted out.

"Are you sure you're okay?" she asked.

"Yes, just tired."

"What does drinking from the Chalice do to you?"

"In general, or me personally? I don't know," he said, and lifted the button hanging around his neck. "Baelhar thought this button might negate the Chalice's restorative power, the way it does magic. I was afraid my tampering with the Olde Magyk might have changed something in me. Something that would have allowed the Chalice to heal me."

Of course he would assume the chalice wouldn't work on the monster.

Before Eleanor could comment, he smiled. "Apparently it was the sword."

"Why?"

"It needed to be removed. However, we both could be sleeping. If you hurry, you might be able to sneak into bed before anyone knows you were gone and makes you answer questions." He smiled. "Like Jack."

Chapter Twenty-Five

ELEANOR STOOD IN THE HAYLOFT. SHE WIPED THE SWEAT from her forehead with one hand and pulled her shirt, which was stuck to her skin, loose with the other. It was hot. Unbearably so.

She watched Flora, who stood with her back to the target they'd made from boards and bales of hay. When Rob gave her the okay, Flora spun and threw the knife. She grinned when it landed within the target's circle with a satisfying sound.

"Better," Rob said. "Don't peek." He waited for her to shut her eyes before he moved the target.

Flora waited patiently. She grinned again at Eleanor.

"'Kay," he said when he'd moved out of range.

Flora spun again and, finding the new spot, let her knife fly. Again, she scored a good hit.

"This time, two," Rob told her, winking at Eleanor and Jack as he'd placed the target flat on the floor. Flora waited for his go-ahead, turned, and threw them, one right after another. His trick didn't faze her. She nailed the target both times.

"By Jove, I think she's got it," Jack said, tugging her braid.

Flora's smile spread, proud of herself.

"Good. Then let's go swimming," Eleanor suggested.

"Sail to Lime?" asked Jack.

"Not for a year or two, but thanks for asking," Rob said.

"Take the horses to the dam?"

"I guess," Jack said.

"The ocean's still too cold, anyway," Rob said. "River's warmer."

"You guys get the horses and put the bridles on," Eleanor said. "I have to run to the house real quick."

Eleanor ran down the loft stairs and passed Patters lying beside the tack room door. She noticed a small pile of remains a few feet away and wrinkled her nose. Some poor creature, identifiable only by its gallbladder, had recently suffered a torturous death.

"No one you know," the cat told her.

"Hi, Patters."

"Shhh!" Patters said.

Eleanor grinned. "Pyskes having their mid-morning nap?"

"Yes, mercifully," Patters said. "The kittens are crazy to catch one—well, three of them are. FatMackerel could care less. With the incessant chatter, though, it's tempting to look the other way."

"Please don't!" Eleanor shuddered.

Patters yawned. "At least that insipid Hob is in the house now."

Eleanor patted the cat on the head and continued to the house. After she retrieved what she needed from her room, Eleanor grabbed beach towels for everyone and headed back to the barn.

Rob, Jack, and Flora waited with the horses. Eleanor gave each their towels, and slid onto Ginger's back from the mounting block.

They ambled out the point road, in no real hurry in the heat. Clayr and Handrven waited by the path to the Lee, and Clayr gave them a little salute. Handrven ignored them.

When they reached the logging road, Jack said, "I wanna see where everything happened."

"It's farther in, near the river. There won't be much to see.

Baelhar and Clayr destroyed the remains of the other Noctivagus."

Jack and Rob looked disappointed. When they reached the spot, they paused to look around, but as Eleanor had stated, only trampled ground remained. They continued to the dam.

As they approached, they heard talking and laughter. Meg and her friends were lying on the rocks. Eleanor recognized Mim, Sheila, Hocke, Foster, and Libbet, but was pleased to see Vidia wasn't present. Two younger girls played at the water's edge.

Meg stood and waved when she heard them approaching. "Hi. We were hoping, since it was so hot, you'd come swimming. We want the scoop!"

Eleanor laughed. "Aren't you worried you'll be seen?"

Foster answered happily, "Nope. Humans don't see us. Anything bad we do will be blamed on you."

Jack grinned. "Hey. I'm Jack. This is Rob and Flora."

Flora slid from Willow's back and led the pony to the younger children.

"We brought Sheila's and Hocke's little sisters, Trina and Lueri, to meet Flora. That, and taking his sister was the only way Hocke could come. He's in trouble for filching the mead," Mim said, laughing.

Hocke bowed, hardly repentant. "Want some? I got more."

Jack grinned.

Rob did too, but said, "Swim, first. It's hot." He rode Sargent into the water, and Ringo and Jack followed.

Eleanor slid from Ginger's back to take off her cutoffs, and felt the bulges in her pockets. She pulled out what she'd brought, walked over to Meg, and held them out to her. "I have a surprise for you."

Meg gave her a questioning look, and then squealed when she saw three bottles of polish in shocking colors. Hot pink, orange, and lime green. Fascinated, Sheila and Mim examined them, their eyes big.

"Let me have a swim and we'll paint our nails," Eleanor told them.

Eleanor climbed on Ginger, and they walked into the water. When the cool water reached the mare's withers, Eleanor slid from the mare's back and swam alongside. Ginger stopped next to Sargent and Ringo, who'd positioned themselves in the current. Before Eleanor could swim to Rob and Jack, Gunnr's presence filled her mind.

"Nice day for a swim."

"It's alive," she said, mimicking Frankenstein.

"You're funny."

"Who sleeps for two days?"

"Were you concerned?"

"Yes. Where are you, anyway?"

"Sitting on the dam."

Eleanor looked toward the dam and smiled when she saw him. He sat in the center, dangling his feet in the water. "Be right back," she told Rob, and swam over.

She treaded water and looked up at him. "Hey."

Gunnr offered his hand and pulled her up beside him.

"All recovered? Really?"

"Yes. Never better."

Moreover, she felt it. He was relaxed and fully recovered. His contentment spread to her.

"Good. But what about Radek?"

"No idea. He'll have to go to ground for a while and heal. I have no idea if he'll stay in this area. Camedon's alerted the other Keepers and the Elders who are here. He'll turn up. We won this battle, but he made it clear we're at war. He'll try again."

Eleanor thought about that, watching Flora play with her new friends beside the river. It was nice, but it was also important. Eleanor understood now why Camedon strove for unity among the Beings of the Realm. Though the children didn't realize it, they were building more than sandcastles.

Gunnr interrupted her thoughts. "I've been wondering about something, though. You never told me what Motte said."

"She didn't really say much. Just that you needed me, but to close my mind to you so you would not be aware of my presence."

He frowned. "But not why?"

"No—wait. Something about the moment deciding time, but I had no idea what she was talking about."

He frowned. "Deciding *Time*? Are you sure that's what she said?"

Eleanor nodded. "What does it mean?"

"I have no idea. I can guess which moment she meant—had your presence not distracted Radek, he would've finished me off and escaped with the Chalice. But I wonder *how* that moment decides Time." He looked into the distance, thinking. He gave his head a little shake, dismissing the Gargoyle's mysterious words, and returned his attention to Eleanor.

But she was curious. "Can't you ask her?"

"I can, but she wouldn't answer, and even if she did, I probably wouldn't understand."

"*You can say that again,*" the Gargoyle's gravelly voice sounded in both of their heads.

"Get out of my head," Eleanor said, annoyed, and closed her mind to the Gargoyle.

A wheezing chuckle slid under Eleanor's defenses. "*Crowded in there?*"

Eleanor felt her withdraw. She shuddered. "I thought you said her attitude would improve."

"I was wrong."

About the Author

THE SECRETS OF THE RED PAINT PEOPLE HAVE HAUNTED Maine for 7000 years. Paige W. Pendleton is busy writing those tales.

About the Artist

THOMAS BLOCK RETIRED AS AN ART EDUCATOR IN COASTAL Maine after 37 years to pursue a career as an artist/illustrator.

His recent books include *"Togus a Coon Cat Finds a Home"* by News Center 6 Don Carrigan and *"Baxter in the Blaine House"* by Blaine House director Paula Benoit. Thomas has illustrated several young adult novels as well, including *" Patch Scratching"* by Steven Powell, and *"The Black Ledge "* series by Paige W. Pendleton.

Thomas lives and works by the sea in Midcoast Maine.

Appendix

Älvkors – Elf Cross carved into the summit of Mount Megunticook. Star-shaped. Each point represents the four Elements, **Earth**, **Air**, **Water**, and **Fire**. The uppermost point represents **Time**.

Rune Stone – The heart of the star-shaped Elf Cross, on which the terms of the ancient Accord between the beings are inscribed.

Solstice Ceremony – The ceremony on the summer solstice on which the terms of the Accord are renewed.

Black Point – Point of land overlooking Camden Harbor. Protected as the Passage is on the point. Gifted to Oliver black and Hazel Harkins when they married.

Black Ledge – The home built by Oliver Black and Hazel Harkins.

Red Paint People – Maine's indigenous people who inhabited New England and Maritime Canada 2,000 to 6,000 years ago. Archeological remains in Maine and Norway suggest Trans-Atlantic travel.

Rachel Parker – A ship, wrecked in a storm centuries ago.

Human Characters

Peter Driscoll – Father. Scientist. Owns Driscoll Pharmacology.

Virginia Driscoll – Mother. Forensic Odontologist.

Rob Driscoll – Age 14

Eleanor Driscoll – Age 13

Jack Driscoll – Age 12

Flora Driscoll – Age 8

Charlotte Black Bradford – Librarian. Daughter of Oliver Black
and Hazel Harkins.

Oliver Black – Father of Charlotte Black Bradford. Deceased.

Hazel Harkins – Mother of Charlotte Black Bradford. Deceased.

Sam Nickerson – Lives in carriage house. Takes care of horses
at Black Ledge Stable.

Katy Snow – Eleanor's best friend, away for the summer.

Realm Characters

Keeper – Diplomatic position in the Realm, identifiable by
ornate cloak.

Ljósálfar – Light Elves

Álfheimr – Kingdom of Light Elves

Dökkálfar – Dark Elves, or Dwarves

Dökkálfaheimr – Kingdom of the Dwarves

Betrayer – Those who participated in the sacrificial ritual.
Are now dependent upon the consumption of iron
from blood.

Night Elves – The Betrayers who choose to return to the light,
and the Realm. They renew the Accord on each
Summer Solstice.

Noctivagi – The Betrayers who embraced the darkness. Wholly
evil. The basis of Vampire legends.

Keepers:

Camedon – Keeper of the Realm

Gladstone – Keeper of British Isles

Astrid – Keeper of Scandinavia

Sveta – Keeper Russia and other Eurasian territory

Light Elves:

Baelhar – Member of Elven Guard

Sehlis – Member of Elven Guard

Azathela – Elven Healer

Handrven – Member of Elven Guard

Maethoron – Member of Elven Guard

Sigildnor – Member of Elven Guard

Solvanha – Elven Queen. Sister of Gunnr

Tahlemar – Member of Elven Guard

Clare – Member of Elven Guard

Dark Elves, or Dwarves:

Vitr – Dwarf King

Lorik – Dwarf murdered by Noctivagus

Betrayer – Those who participated in the sacrificial ritual.

Night Elves:

Gunnr – Member of the Elven Royal family and brother to Queen Solvanha. Acknowledged Elder of the Night Elves, and a Warrior of the Realm.

Lassar

Koravel

Ilus

Noctivagi:

Eilvain – One of the original participants of the sacrificial ritual.

Haflings:

Ralph the Goblin – lives in cellar of Black Ledge. Tends the gardens and grounds.

Floyd the Hob – Assumed residence of Black Ledge with Hob ritual.

Pyskes:

Felix – Pyske

Trinket – Pyske

Fleck – Pyske, daughter of Felix and Trinket

Motte – Gunnr's Gargoyle

Brownies:

Brighty – The head housekeeper of Black Ledge

Martin – Martha's brother

Martha – Martin's sister

Sea Dragon:

Nob, the Great Midgard Serpent of Penobscot Bay

Acadian Water Witch:

Doris – Lives on Lime Island

Do-gakw-ho-wad:

Simo – Abenaki man captured by Eilvain in *The Keeper and the Rune Stone*.

Water Sprites:

Meg – Water Sprite of Megunticook Lake

Sheila – Trina's older sister

Vidia

Mim

Trina – Sheila's younger sister

Fae:

Libbet

Hocke – Lueri's older brother

Foster

Lueri – Hocke's younger sister

Animal Characters

Horses:

Sargent – Large dark brown hunter recently moved to Back Point from Viriginia.

Mack – Chestnut gelding from the South Shore

Ringo – Appaloosa gelding from Texas

Hala – Black Arabian mare from Kentucky

Ginger – Palomino mare from California. Mute.

Willow – Silver pony from California.

Agnes – Crow who resides on Black Point.

Patters Felis Catus – Maine Coon Cat. Resides in Black Point Stable with her kittens, Bing, Kipper, Fossie, and FatMackerel.

Seaton – Seal who lives on the ledges surrounding Curtis Island Light.

24191288R10113

Made in the USA
Charleston, SC
18 November 2013